I0652098

William Hudson

The Dream of Agnoscens

A Poem of the Times

William Hudson

The Dream of Agnoscens
A Poem of the Times

ISBN/EAN: 9783744763516

Printed in Europe, USA, Canada, Australia, Japan

Cover: Foto ©Andreas Hilbeck / pixelio.de

More available books at **www.hansebooks.com**

THE DREAM OF AGNOSCENS

THE DREAM OF AGNOSCENS: A POEM OF THE TIMES. By the REV. W. HUDSON.—EASTBOURNE: Printed for the Author by W. Given, Junction Road. Pp. viii. 248, Fcp. 8vo., Limp Cloth. Price 3/6.

[Post Free from the Author or the Printer.]

THIS Poem has been printed for private circulation. I hope to publish it in due time after a possible revision. The extent of the revision will depend in some degree on the opinions and the criticisms with which I may be favoured by readers. I have attempted to state and characterise the nature, the working, and the results of current systems and opinions, of that "modern thought" whose tumult and contradiction are to many utterly confusing. Such an attempt is attended with difficulty; and I am not quite free from doubt as to one or two features which the critical reader will find. While I am not conscious of having followed any example in the production of the book, I am aware that, in this respect, peculiarity may work to my disadvantage, the form which the thought has taken being uneven.

The Poem is designed to teach the doctrines of Divine Providence, the ministry of angels, and the mystery of sin; to show the profanity of irreverence, the necessity of revelation to the stability of morals, and the insufficiency of opinion; to illustrate the power of the claims of Christ, the protective grace of the Christian life even in connection with intellectual mediocrity (Section vi. " Home"), and the final victory of faith; and to bring into view the certainty of the promises of God. The Poem ends with a speculative glimpse at the glories of the future. The feeling of monotony, which hinders the study of didactic verse, may have been relieved by constant change of metre, though this will not be pleasing to all readers. Under the conviction that—

"A verse may find him who a sermon flies."

I have chosen for my argument the form that seemed most likely to gain me a hearing. The representatives of Agnosticism, Evolution, Pessimism, the Worthlessness of Life, Prayerless Culture, and that Criticism which destroys faith in thinkers as well as faith in God, cannot be named here. But the intelligent reader will be his own guide.

W. HUDSON.

60, PEVENSEY ROAD, EASTBOURNE,
April 2nd, 1889.

THE

DREAM OF AGNOSCENS

A Poem of the Times

BY

WILLIAM HUDSON

Watchman, what of the Night?

EASTBOURNE

PRINTED FOR THE AUTHOR

By W. Given, Junction Road

1889

THIS POEM

IS INSCRIBED TO

MY FRIEND,

GILBERT PURVIS, ESQ., OF LONDON,

IN REMEMBRANCE OF

PLEASANT DAYS ON THE DEEP.

23 January, 1889.

ἦ πολλὰ βροτοῖς ἔστιν ἰδοῦσιν
γνῶναι· πρὶν ἰδεῖν δ'οὐδεὶς μάντις
τῶν μελλόντων ὅ τι πράξει.

Soph. Ajax.

CONTENTS.

Contents.

THE DREAM OF AGNOSCENS.

THE BOOK.

I.

The form's irregular as is the thought
  Of this great age of noisy men, who walk,
    They deem, in wisdom when, judged by their talk,
They are but changelings all.   Ne'er have they sought
Instruction at the fount divine, ne'er bought
  The truth with pain of toil.   Wonder no more
    They are, like waves which dash on yonder shore,
Restless.   There is a faith whereby is brought
To youth, to years, pure good, yea, lasting rest,
  The wealth of innocence, in tempests calm,
    In darkness light, and in distress relief,
With all the joys wherewith the saints are blessed.
  Carry, O book, to some, the healing balm,
    A faithful message of thy ends the chief.

II.

Know thou, O friend, this book may be misread.
  Hast heard the legend told where I have been ?
  What it for me hath meant may here be seen.
The truth, 'tis said, lies deep. Search what is said,
And watch, nor by the legend be deceived.
  Judge not of form before thou dost begin
  To trace the progeny of English sin.
Hast thou once seen what in the lair's conceived ?
  Then be thou warned, and go, and spread alarm,
That those whom thou canst aid may be preserved.
Ah, hast thou seen too much ? Then help thy bard
  To tell the truth and break bold error's charm.
Conviction strong his trembling hand hath nerved ;
Should love of ease an honest aim retard?

THE DREAMER.

Agnoscens dreams ! Billows of darkness roll
Around his life.   Closed is the body's sense
In all its five (or fifty) forms, nor wave
Material can reach the spirit, deep
Involved in fathomless confusion.   Through
His nature creeps an awful pulse, not sense,
But deep and mystic apprehension keen.
With loud and louder roar the vision rolls
Along, if roar that may be called which none
Can hear.   O depth immense of mystery !
He dreams, but what nor voice nor pen can tell.
Himself knows not, and yet would fain declare,
For when the vision passes he is left
Helpless and dull.   He knows not that he dreamed
Of hell and heaven, of earth and paradise,
Of men and women here and everywhere,
Of ease and pain, of prayer and blasphemy,
And sighings in a pit for light of day,

And contradictions loud of men and fiends.

Then why should I, who saw his frame convulsed,

And heard, dismayed, his horror-speaking voice,

And caught some words confused, and syllabled

Their sense, not sing, as through my lyre the muse

Directs, that those who know and yet know not

They know, and boast man never knows at all,

May, hearing, feel Agnoscens dreams the truth?

What is the purport of this timely dream?

Dreamers are many, but how few are seers!

O for that vision which interpreteth.

Agnoscens then will not have dreamed in vain,

Nor bear for naught the name of him that knows.

I.—THE INVISIBLE WORLD.

Agnoscens soars. Beyond the stars deep thought
Sees and reveals the invisible, and hears
The march of those who minister to man,
Discerning forms to human sense unknown.
Agnoscens dreams he, knowing, worships God.
Why waiteth any for the aid of dreams?

MINISTERING SPIRIT.

At Thy command, O Lord, we wing our way,
Joyful to serve for Thee the heirs of life.
The days are evil, and Thy witness mourns.
Yet all the earth hath not forsaken Thee.
The lover of Thy truth in wisdom walks ;
But forms and names conceal Satanic cheat
From such as willingly are led astray,
While lying promises the false deceive,
And through the world is heard the voice of woe.

SECOND MINISTERING SPIRIT. ·

The jovial south loves poesy and song ;
The meditative east is dying old ;
The boastful north now fosters vain deceits ;
The fearless west would let Thy captives go ;
And all in sighs confess their want of Thee.
Thy holy word, contemned, is judged unheard ;
Thy works, misread, are teaching some to scorn ;

And Thy authority is set at naught,
While contradictions load the unwilling ear.
Where men supposed idolatry was dead,
Thy creature, loved before Thee, is adored.
Souls, darkened with profanity, pretend
To lead their fellows in the paths of light.
The poet's song, perverted, serves not Thee,
Nor bears to man the good by Thee designed.
Sweet words, pure lives, and sacred ministries
The sons of men despise, and in their place
Set lies, and vice, and hate, and injury.
Men's hearts are failing for the fear that spreads ;
Thy Church, long waiting, dews her couch with tears ;
And through all lands Thy saints cry day and night
To Thee, their helper in the hour of pain.

THIRD MINISTERING SPIRIT.

The paths of lawlessness Thy foes have strewn
With flowers, to lure the heedless far astray ;
And evil teaching wins the wayward heart,
While Satan prompts the foolish child to roam ;
Though he may hear the counsel of the wise,
And keen rebuke of conscience, oft renewed.
The prayer of godliness I heard, which rose
In solemn cadence on the midnight air,
Thy saint afraid of foes too near, too strong.
Thine answer came, but ruthless deeds were done
By such as chose to serve the tyrant-god.
I saw a tempter rise, in human form,
To lead a child away to pleasing sin,

And in my heart was sorrow at the sight,
Such sorrow as is felt in angel-breasts.
The work I watched, as one another drew
To deep and deeper sin, himself the while
Stricken in heart with sense of guilt and woe,
With hate, and rage, and shame; and I had wept
For pity, if to me tears had belonged.
His swift advance I marked, from ill to worse,
And saw him slain, at length, with his own hand.
He met his doom with terror filled. O Lord,
His guides and teachers Thou wilt judge, not we.
O let the victims of his spreading sin
At Thy most gracious hands seek mercy, Lord ;
And suffer me to help the wandering feet
To find the path which leads the faithful home.
This is Thy servants' pure delight, while woe
Is eloquent on earth through every land,
Since fierce iniquity is master still.
When comes the end of this deep mystery ?

THE LORD.

Ye minister to them who choose My will,
Your joy at My command to serve the saved.
The prayers of righteous men with Me prevail,
And Satan, conquered, sees his kingdom fall.
Beneath My feet all foes shall be subdued.
I wait the promise, sure to be fulfilled.
The day is dawning which shall see the truth
Supreme with all. It shall prevail, in love
To friends in heaven, in wrath to foes in hell.

These forfeit life, by grace no more restrained,
And sink in woe, by their own sin o'erwhelmed ;
But those have joy eternal, by free gift,
Sought in the prayer of faith and penitence.
Go ye, and minister to all the heirs
Of My salvation.   Grace directs your way ;
And ye shall see the wealth of love divine,
Shall hear the witness of eternal right,
Shall justify the power which conquers sin,
And share the bliss of human souls redeemed,
That bliss which grows to all eternity,
The gift of Him who sits upon the throne.

CHORUS OF MINISTERING SPIRITS.

Speed we past the glowing suns
    On the errands of Thy grace ;
Swift as light our service runs
    When we aid the needy race.

Man's foul foe, victorious,
    Acts the tyrant to this hour ;
But he ne'er hath conquered us,
    And he shall lose all his power,
As the faithful of the race,
    Strengthened with redeeming care,
His vile usurpation chase,
    Helped by us the toil to bear.

In the conflict and the pain
    Of life's short and feverish day,
Those who love Thee, Lord, would fain
    Leave the earth and soar away

To the rest for saints prepared.
  Till the conflict finds its end,
We, who in their pain have cared,
  We will all their steps attend.

Well they know when saints are weak
  They have Thy sufficient strength,
Who wilt lead the truly meek,
  Till they conquer all at length.

When oppressed with sense of need,
  Prayer they make their loved employ,
To their side for Thee to speed,
  Is for us a peerless joy.

Prompt we thought to cheer the heart
  Of Thy servants in distress ;
Help to choose the better part
  Them that walk the wilderness ;

Guard the faithful on the way
  Where through danger they must go ;
Hold them up as dawns the day
  When they leave all things below.

Let us speed then past the stars,
  Bearing messages unknown ;
Naught this joyous service mars,
  Ever loyal to Thy throne.

Now unknown, but soon revealed,
  These our messages of care ;
Naught from Thee is e'er concealed,
  God, who rulest everywhere.

Saints are learning now Thy mind,
    Sojourning on earth below ;
When they here their treasure find,
    Heaven's own wonders they shall know.

II.—A GARDEN.

The bound sublime from starry depths to earth
No shock Agnoscens gives. The path of dreams
Is anywhere. But when his soul entranced
Touches in thought this sphere of flesh and blood,
How all is changed! Men and their aims pass by
In aspect clear. And now Agnoscens walks
Where sorrow lives at home. He hears, distressed,
The grieving of a soul to sin betrayed.
So grieves the bleating lamb lost on the moor,
No shepherd near, while .wintry tempests howl.
Quick flow the tears that none is nigh to stem,
And deep that heart-break which no balm can heal.
How vast the mercy that can save the worst.

Margaret. Richard. Stephanas.

MARGARET.

Straying sheep, through broken hedges,
    Led, can find an easy way;
Children, lured among the sedges,
    Late were drowned in yonder bay.
Woe is me; the fence was broken
    When we strayed across the lea;
I believed the falsehood spoken;
    Still it clings, a curse, to me.

Guards surround the well-conducted,
　Promptings they at once repress ;
Me, alas, had none instructed,
　Easy, therefore, was access.
Woe is me ; the guard removèd
　Soon I went from ill to worse ;
Though the inward voice reprovèd,
　Nor was hid the coming curse.

Virtue is a plant so tender
　It may wither at a breath ;
Wretch is he and base pretender
　Who can do what works its death.
Woe is me ; I weep and tremble,
　Anguish eats my flesh away ;
What my miseries resemble
　I, in words, can never say.

STEPHANAS.

One there is who all things knoweth ;
　He will her avenger be.
Destiny for ever groweth ;
　She may yet deliverance see.
Bliss for woe, and good for evil,
　She may yet in mercy find,
If she will renounce the devil
　And no more be led as blind.

MARGARET.

My life I mourn from day to day ;
　I weep till all my strength is spent ;

My enemies have much to say,
  Who know the way I weakly went
In days of unprotected youth.
  Have they much better been controlled ?
Ah, they are very pure, forsooth,
  Nor tempters have, of purpose bold !
Let them despise me more and more,
  I am beneath themselves so far ;
But what if I myself restore,
  And they their virtuous beauty mar ?
But, Oh, how weak ! can I withstand
  Wiles, craft, and lies, if they return ?
Conscience hath made me understand
  In what dread sense a soul may burn.
O God, what can a sinner do,
  Who would be saved but knows not how ?
My very being I shall rue ;
  Clouds of thick gloom are o'er me now.

STEPHANAS.

Oh, do not seek excuse for sin,
But hear the voice that speaks within,
Condemning all that brings you shame ;
And for your fault no other blame.

MARGARET.

I hear your words and gladly listen.

RICHARD.

Were it not dark, you'd see there glisten
Two tearful eyes.

STEPHANAS.

    And her breast heaves,
Because a guilty conscience grieves.

MARGARET.

It pains my heart and turns my head
To know how true what I have said.
Surely some course for me is right ;
What shall I do to find the light ?
Loud speaks to-day the voice within ;
And no excuse I seek for sin.
Who offers mercy to the worst
May save me still from things accursed.
But I have left the path of truth,
Nay, I am ruined, in my youth.

STEPHANAS.

I shall believe your words sincere
When you display that wholesome fear
   Which guards the truly wakened soul.
Then take no more the crooked way
Wherein you have, from day to day,
   Refused all good and wise control.

Infirmity's the name for sin,
With those who would approval win
   For things which truth divine condemns ;
But black to white can not be turned,
Howe'er the truth's denied or spurned,
   By one who purity contemns.

A day of gloom before you lies,
And bitter tears must flood your eyes,
   Ere peace and strength can be restored ;
But when you pray with pure intent,
Your soul entire on virtue bent,
   You'll find the grace you have implored.

When you invoked the holy name,
Confessing what has caused you shame,
   I heard with joy the strain of prayer,
And with you mourned o'er what has been.
As I your woe have, pitying, seen,
   So I beseech to shun the snare.

RICHARD.

You may think me the snare that has fettered her feet,
   But such thinking's erroneous, I ween,
For the walk o'er the lea had its record complete
   Long before I her face had once seen.
When she says they betrayed her, I cannot be meant,
   Nor with that will I burden my soul,
For the fence was all broken, whate'er her intent ;
   And I found she had no self-control.
But she stepped o'er my path and a tempter became
   At a time when I, weak as herself,
In my walk could be hindered as traveller lame,
   Or attracted as miser by pelf.
If her weakness you pity, I pity it too,
   And to such a one I will be kind ;
But to me 'tis unfair to be blamed for what grew
   In a weak uncontrollable mind.

STEPHANAS.
'Tis error's part
To reason so,
For one whose smart
Of guilt is woe.

Sure thou didst see
She lacked control
When purity
Had lost its soul.

It is no ghost
That haunteth thee,
Now blamed the most
For cruelty.

Go where thou wilt,
Justice will bind
Thy load of guilt ;
Nor canst thou find

For Margaret's thrall
One poor defence ;
For over all
Is Providence.

Nor knave nor fool
Can e'er evade
The powers that rule
O'er all things made.
Man must repent
Or lack content.

RICHARD.

More have you said than I can hear with ease ;
But, pleased myself, I care not you to please ;
My doctrine is defined, and I stand here
To say, Of such fine talk I have no fear.
Let parsons preach, and moralists display
What is, how proudly, called the light of day ;
Let Christians dream of truth divine and bliss,
Then, boasting, tell of benefits we miss,
Who cast away their doctrines, and bestow
Our chief regard on that which man should know ;
Let orthodoxy shout its virtuous creed,
To prove that for our way of life no need
Has yet been shewn ; let curse be heaped on curse
For those who go, 'tis said, from bad to worse ;
Let Margaret blame me as I know she may,
Though I but walk in her own chosen way ;
Yea, let my words be heard with deep disdain,
While no one cares if I have loss or pain ;
What matters it ? What prate they all about ?
I will keep calm, and boldly reason out
My course.   Fools mock at sin ; but I'm no fool.
What they call sin is but, to me, the tool
Wherewith is done a work that else were not.
Though Churches fall and creeds and systems rot,
What care I, just allowed to please myself ?
Dull prudence I will lay upon the shelf.
Divinity and all this vapouring talk
To me are naught ; in my own path I walk.
Who is my master ? Am I not my own ?

B

'Tis said that men will reap what they have sown.
When will they reap and where ? If no man knows,
Need it give pain to dream that each thing grows
Which I have done ? Who tends it till the time
Of reaping ? One to guard each separate clime,
Or one for all ? I do not comprehend ;
Nor will I now my liberty defend
With aught but practice. I will wait for all
That orthodoxy proves must me befall.
Shew me a better way, and make it clear
'Tis better, that I then my course may steer
By new-made chart. Meanwhile, reprover, cease,
And let me please myself and live in peace.
My mind is fixed ; the course is clear as day ;
Let me leave you to ponder what I say.
When I have gone, Margaret may dry her tears ;
But, know ye both, I have no craven fears.

STEPHANAS.

Well, let him take his chosen way.
The more I hope to see the day
        When thou wilt find
        Both heart and mind
Set free from all the snares,
Of thoughts perverse and hurtful cares,
        That bind thee now.
        Repenting, bow
        To Him who hears
        The prayer of tears.

Forget not what thou well hast known,
That each must reap as she has sown.

    Give up thy youth
    To walk in truth
    And purity.
    All vanity
    Be ended here;
    And in God's fear
Be passed the time that yet remains.
    Ere I withdraw
    Heed thou this law :
Who conquers self true victory gains,
And good above all price retains.

MARGARET.

Dark the day that saw my fall;
Strong the fetters that enthral;
Dim my vision of the way
When 'tis told me yet I may
    Be restored.
Keen the sense that I have sinned;
Tempests like a mighty wind
Shake me to my central soul;
O that I had self-control.
    God, adored
By the faithful and the pure,
Why must I these qualms endure ?
Conscience to a dungeon throws
One who, sinning, better knows !
    How deplored

By the friends who love me best,
And have oft with tears caressed,
Should I end this piercing strife
With the forfeit of my life !
       Like a sword
Sin is piercing now my heart.
What can bid my woe depart ?
Why am I so full of fear
Standing solitary here,
On me the All-seeing Eye ?
God alone my tears can dry.

III.—A WEST-END CLUB.

Agnoscens dreams that he is sitting
  With sages of the day,
And hears them talk, each other hitting,
  And whiles his time away.
  All are too great to pray !
Could any soul, taught as this dreamer,
  Be with wise talk content ?
As soon would peace come to the schemer
  Ever on wiles intent.

Dardan. Phane. Aretas. Hermes. Voices.

DARDAN.

Should I say I could ride on the wings of the wind
  O'er mountain and forest and sea,
Or tell you I could grasp with the strength of my mind
  The meaning of all shewn to me,
You'd behold in my looks, as I sat on this chair,
  Or hear in my tones as I spoke,
My confession the doctrine much needed repair;
  And me you would bid all revoke.

ARETAS.

Let sense with all your sound combine,
And make it lustrous as is mine.

PHANE.

Else what is all the boasting worth
That goes like water spilt on earth ?

HERMES.

Let us be men of sober mind,
And guidance in pure science find.

A VOICE.

But what if ye are all mistaken ?
'Twill be my work your minds to waken.

DARDAN.

Well, I teach no such folly as what I have said,
  But always keep sense in my view.
I am glad to consent by the Pope to be led,
  For doctrine that's true is not new ;
And to him, by consent of the wisest of all,
  Is granted infallible skill ;
'Tis untrue that he holds in unchristian thrall
  The people who bow to his will.

PHANE.

When words are strong, and sense is weak,
The speaker still hath truth to seek.

DARDAN.

Of the Councils' decrees I have nothing to say ;
  I think Inquisitions are dead ;
But the Catholic Church knows the only right way,
  And I by its guides will be led ;

And the reason for this is the fact that I doubt
    If the protest, so called, can exist,
When the winds of new science are blowing about,
    Dispersing all doctrinal mist.
But I must have some doctrine to help me to live,
    Because it is made to appear
Nothing else that this world to a man has to give
    Is worthy of hope or of fear ;
And yet sometimes I think 'twould be better by far
If new science were taken as sole guiding star ;   [alarm ?
But then what could be done should the Church feel
I must promptly fall back to recant and disarm.

A Voice.

Velvet coat and golden eyeglass,
    Fashion's glove, and patent shoe,
Wine, tobacco, and the high mass
    Comfort yield to such as you.
One has proved with show of logic,
    Life's not worth the living now ;
But the age is demagogic,
    And men know both why and how ;
And he has not proved his point
By a logic out of joint.
Should he try to do it better,
He would but himself enfetter.

Hermes.

Light beams from far, and we behold, in paths
Where sages walk, things which all sense transcend.
Philosophy was born to bless mankind,

And science now attends as handmaid fair
In form complete, of vision clear and keen ;
Religion meanwhile cringing in decay.
When mind first strove to interpret what appeared,
The seed was sown whose fruit we now behold.
How long the time of growth no man can know.
Men dreamed of ghosts, believed they were alive,
Though they were naught but fancies of the brain,
And then adored them all.   The names, or loved
Or hated, of their ancestors were still
Mild benefactors or avengers dire,
Whom 'twas impiety not to adore.
Thus did religion grow to those grotesque,
Yea, hideous, forms which now appear where men
Like us, of scientific light, have told
The truth, laid bare the shameless cheat, and poured
Meet scorn on errors that have cursed the world.
One Cause there may be.   Who can tell ?   Not I,
Nor all the doctors.   We wish not to know.
Yet we can prove our views are right for all.
True wisdom is, as men by us are taught.

A VOICE.

To you incomprehensibility
Is sweet as native air ; in it ye thrive.
Your temple is a phantom seen through mist.
And, in pure sunshine, would not once appear.
Ye boast of light.   What may it be ?   Ye give
The sacred name to clouds of doubt and fogs
Of speculation, which will pass away,

As mountain mists are melted by the sun,
When dawns the morn whose light is heavenly truth.
One Cause original, made known in all
His works, the homage claims of intellect,
Bidding the thinker pray, that he may feel
Who worships not is but a part of man.
Pray then, O sage, and know thy majesty,
The fulness of a manhood pure and free.
So set thy feet upon the rock of strength.

HERMES.

Authority is all within ourselves.

A VOICE.

Ye came to know but yesterday.

HERMES.

Alas,
Men knew not in the ancient days what now
Is known ; but they have palmed on us a cheat
Of ghosts, which this bright age detects and casts
Away.

A VOICE.

But they had faith and used it well,
And died.   Ye too shall die ; and days will come
When ye shall stand among the ancient names
To make men wonder that ye had no faith,
No knowledge meet of truth divine, no light,
No fellowship with Him who gave your all.

HERMES.

Vain superstitions we discard, to build
On facts alone.   The old beliefs must die.
Erelong no man will know their wrinkled face ;
And when they all have passed, to be no more,
The sciences will flourish in their stead.

A VOICE.

Clear up the facts, and shew your doctrine true.

ARETAS.

Truth rises, Oh, how slowly, into sight.
The generations come and go ; but man
Divine, remains and cannot die.   Creeds fade
And Churches mourn, but we have full content.
Divine humanity is our true God.
Humanity we worship, as is due.

A VOICE.

Hath not sense gone with old discarded creeds ?
For man is weak, and, worshipped, still has needs.

DARDAN.

Man's needs are met when he obeys the Church.
This has been proved with labour and research.

HERMES.

But all the Churches contradict the creed,
Teaching what sorely mocks man's deepest need.

DARDAN.

One Church there is that never has been changed ;
And on her side all thinking must be ranged.
No right to think what she has not required,
What her authority has not inspired.

ARETAS.

The truth, made clear at last, we publish now,
Calling on cultured souls with us to bow
To great humanity, the worshipful,
Wherein must ever shine the light men need.
Come, learn, we say, what worship is and where
'Tis given aright, that each may have a share.

PHANE.

What worship ye ? Which of the faiths professed
Directs your course ? Are ye all right, or is
The truth divided ? Ye can not agree,
But fiercely fight in view of all the town.
The Church once fought, but now can live in peace,
Her controversies hushed in calm content,
Her energy employed in works of love
And charitable thought. Ye say the Church
Must die of strife, and bid her watch herself.
But how ye strive, and fret to find no peace !
This is a sight which men of thought observe,
A sight which anxious souls can not forget ;
True wisdom would your vain disputes control.
Be wise, and feel the vanity of strife ;
Be wise to day, nor waste your strength and time.

A VOICE.

This wrangling palls.
Mere manhood calls
    For reconciliation.
Ye might agree
The means to see
    Which made your own great nation.
Ye know that love
For things above
    Hath ruled your education;
And after all
'Tis very small
    Ye feel such provocation,
When o'er the past
Your glance is cast
    In search of condemnation
For those who find,
In heart and mind,
    Through Christ true elevation.
When things are seen in science-light,
Ye will not thus each other fight.

PHANE.

Shocked is intelligence at what is seen.
Our books are read with laughter by divines
Whose insight keen detects the cheat of words.
We might agree to end their boastful scorn.
We who infallibilities contemn
And all old creeds, still fight to prove our own,
Though they have sprung as mushrooms from the ground

The newest systems we now contradict
And overthrow. Are we the men to kill
Religions and their place supply with thought
Of man, more just, more true ?   What have we seen ?
Where once raged war reigns peace to day, and strife
Is hot where we the works of peace could boast.
Why live we thus ?   It is a sight to make
'Ashamed.   My counsel is, Be reconciled,
Nor shew divines our sciences at war,
Nor waste that strength which should pursue the truth,
Nor falsify the boast that makes us proud.

HERMES.

I know the truth and can not yield
To other men my hard-won field.
They will attain if they but let
My doctrines in their minds be set.

ARETAS.

Your views have lost their charm for me ;
I can not in your boast agree,
And have no patience with divines.
Wisdom, for me, in manhood shines.
Humanitarianism is right ;
For that alone I mean to fight.

PHANE.

Ye fight indeed to little good.
As well shoot flies in yonder wood ;
The more ye shoot, they swarm the thicker.
Oh, reason not like men in liquor ;

But honestly admit ye err
In your hot bustle, boast, and stir ;
For tearing old religions down
The laughing-stock of all the town.

A VOICE.

I told you once, and tell again,
Ye great infallibles are men
　　Who put forth strength,
To try to bring each other down ;
Your strife's the talk of all the town ;
　　Be calm at length.

For when ye thus have done your best,
And riddles great and small have guessed,
　　And taught by books,
Ye have not traced the secret out,
Which on you from all things about
　　For ever looks.

It looks as when your reverent sires
Assembled round their sacred fires
　　To worship—what ?
They had a faith which ruled their lives ;
But faith, ye think, now scarce survives,
　　And soon will not.

Have ye no faith ? Can any man
The heavens or earth one moment scan,
　　Or look within,
And not need faith ? What's known is known ;
But ye with labour have but shewn
　　The fog ye're in.

There is a light for men whose souls
The love of truth divine controls ;
    They grace receive.
Should that pure love your spirits rule,
And discipline your nature school,
    Ye would believe.

Ye do believe what men declare,
Who lay the facts of matter bare
    And classify.
Jesus, be sure, hath done so much ;
Nay, He doth your deep spirits touch,
    For ever nigh.

His knowledge ye would not dispute,
His reasons ye can not confute,
    Ye know His claim ;
Why kick ye then against the prongs,
Denying what to you belongs ?
    Stop, stop, for shame !

IV.—A BROAD HEATH.

Agnoscens wanders o'er the heath,
　　Dreaming and dreaming more.
At first above and then beneath,
　　Behind, and then before,
He thinks he hears a warning spoken,
　　And would attend,
　　But voices blend,
As fancy walks with sober men ;
　　And still he dreams and dreams again ;
Nor is the spell one moment broken.

Richard.   Stephanas.   Margaret.   Lucidus.   Carolus.
Lucia.   Voices.

RICHARD.

We meet for pleasure, and are free,
Right glad we thus each other see ;
Broad is the heath and bright the day ;
All sadness let us drive away.

LUCIDUS.

Who taste the sweets that letters give,
And they alone, have learned to live ;
No man can his full height attain
If he uncultured will remain.

If letters ruled as they should rule,
The race would put itself to school,
And we should see an end of strife
In this our sad and transient life.

CAROLUS,

That culture which the mind attains
Is naught, if man in heart remains
Still unrenewed.   Seek grace divine.
O may its light be ever mine.

MARGARET.

So spoke I once, but speak not now.

LUCIA.

If 'twas but speaking, Margaret, how
Could you expect that saving grace
Which shines in the believer's face ?

MARGARET.

What I expect is known to me,
And you shall not my teacher be.
I have no mind with you to jest,
But know the course that suits me best.

LUCIA.

Then take the course that's wise and safe.
Else wilfulness your soul will chafe,
And many a tear, in secret shed,
Will tell how you are now misled.

c

A VOICE.

They come again,
Women and men,
To take their walk,
And freely talk,
  Just as they choose.

Open to-day
Is yonder way,
Though there once stood
Gate strong and good.
  Themselves some lose.

RICHARD.

Though I knew ye were speaking, since voices I heard,
Yet the meaning has reached me of never a word.
My attention was claimed by some thoughts of my own,
And the drift of my thinking shall promptly be shewn.
Life is lightened with comfort or burdened with pain ;
And I will have my pleasure, though health may be slain.
They have proved it at last, as I said that they would,
Just as surely as this is the way to the wood,
Yea, have proved the old notions all worthless and wrong,
And invited to joyance in letters and song.
They have shewn us how happy a man may become
And of their ripest doctrine I read you the sum :—

  Let him tell us in a trice
  What is virtue, what is vice.
  I claim pleasure ; must I suffer
  Just because the creed's a cuffer ?

That's my virtue which is sweet ;
In me, deed and doctrine meet ;
Creeds are nonsense ;   that is certain ;
All I crave is a thick curtain.

A Voice.

Oh, remember, thou, so wise,
Darkness hides not from all eyes.

Richard.

Where the hand that more can free us ?
Whose the eye that cares to see us ?
Our own pastimes, sense has told us,
Are the things which now should hold us.
Vice is in the needless thrall
Vain old nonsense casts o'er all.

A Voice.

Though so safe in thine own eyes,
Mischief straight before thee lies.

Lucia.

I heard a voice, of warning tone,
Speaking not for myself alone.

Margaret.

I heard, but care not what it said ;
I am not by such trifles led.

Lucia.

It bids me pause, and brings a fear
Of ills which may to me be near.

MARGARET.

I wonder you yourself molest ;
Be still, and let your feelings rest.

LUCIA.

Not one step further will I go,
Unless I first your purpose know.

MARGARET.

Go home, then ; whisper to your mother,
A feeling which you could not smother
Has brought you back from friends to-day,
Who go without you on their way.

LUCIA.

I go ; for I have heard that voice
  Which speaks for virtue, truth, and God,
Bid me withdraw and, saved, rejoice,
  Or bear, with pain, correction's rod.
Conscience I instantly obey,
And leave you and your chosen way.

MARGARET.

She will be safe when I am lost,
In storms of condemnation tossed.

RICHARD.

Lucia has gone, afraid to stay,
Afraid of danger on this way.
Danger lives near to feeble minds,
And one who seeks it quickly finds ;
But we are strong and guard our own
Content to reap as we have sown.

MARGARET.

My friend, afraid, goes home to tell
  Her tale of something she has heard ;
For me, be sure, it were not well
  To do a thing quite so absurd.
I laughed, I jeered, but could not move
  Her mind from what had been resolved.
But can we her bad thoughts disprove,
  And shew we're in no ill involved ?

RICHARD.

We cannot live with those who dry
Our lives to arid sands, and try
To rob us of our joy. I'm free ;
This all my friends shall surely see.
If Lucia come with us no more
And never friendship's breach restore,
With pious talk we can dispense,
To follow sober common sense.
When freedom all my powers ungirds,
  My thoughts outrun my swiftest words,
And all my reckonings are in surds ;
But I am my own master still,
And mean to follow what I will.
Come, Lucidus, read your new song,
And this our flowing joy prolong.

LUCIDUS.

Light and sweetness, man's true treasure,
  Give to him the purest pleasure ;

Lucid thinking, graceful style,
Please for ever, not a while ;
And where literary art is,
It must charm all sober parties.

Pained I am beyond expression
When the learned make confession,
Culture, books, and writing fine
Suffer still their souls to pine ;
For to me it is a wonder
Bliss and letters keep asunder.

We are told of mighty sages
Striving as men toil for wages ;
Let them stop, agree, and find,
In the fruits of cultured mind,
That which is the only pleasure
Worth the spending of their treasure.

CAROLUS.

The song is dry
But dims the eye
With tears which are not sweet.
I like to see,
Because, for me,
The head must guide the feet.

But what is said
To clear the head
And shew men how they need ?
The praise of light,
For souls not right,
Is darksome work indeed.

Letters are good,
As yonder wood
Has timber for the using ;
But man is sad
Who would be glad
But for his sore abusing

Of precious things.
Away he flings
God's word of free salvation.
Let Jesus reign ;
Else all in vain
Light, sweetness, elevation.

Who sing of light
But have not might
To stem the tide of passion,
For lack of strength
Must sink at length,
O'erwhelmed beyond compassion.

Then learn the strains
Which faith maintains,
Ineffable for sweetness,
And thou shalt find,
In heart and mind,
Light, and for heaven a meetness.

RICHARD.

I like not your preaching, I like not your song ;
You have hindered us with them already too long.
And we now mean to leave you. We know the way well

CAROLUS.

And the path they have chosen has led some to hell.

LUCIDUS.

Let dogmatism hold its foul breath,
And not consign one soul to death.
What right have you to say the word
Which from your lips I just have heard ?
The doom of souls is God's affair ;
Let no weak mortal ever dare
His judgment to anticipate.
Touch not the secret things of fate.

STEPHANAS.

I touch no secret things, but talk of light,
Using your words in other sense.   Be true
To Him who bled on that effulgent cross
Whose light makes clear for man the path to heaven.
Who walks not in that light wends from his weal.
Though culture sit on his exalted brow
His steps to guide.   Delusive light hath him
To blindness brought ; and now he walks as one
Who knows nor where to go nor how to move.
He lives content on meaner fare when Christ
Would give the best.   Compare the light of faith,
Seen in the modesty of Lucia's love,
And in her firm rebuke of wilfulness.
By treacherous song and flippant boast alarmed,
She fled as flees for liberty a slave.
Her conscious soul, made sensitive by love
Of truth, refused to breathe the poisoned air

Of thoughts untrue, impure, and deeds forbidden.
Where none seemed safe, exposed to Satan's darts,
Assailed by thoughts which uninvited come,
And go not when the conscience bids them go,
. She could not, would not, stay. We know her well,
A pattern to the young of every home.
More than was her design she now hath done,
Done here what all should promptly imitate.
Hers is not vain philosophy which knows
No check for sin, no need for prayer, no God.
Light she will have wherever duty calls,
And sweetness is the breath of her pure life.
But what remains for those who Christ deny ?
Thick gloom for life, black midnight for the tomb,
But Memphian darkness for the land beyond.

V.—A THICK WOOD.

———

Darkness from mortal eyes can hide
　　What light to shame delivers.
Agnoscens dreams, and at his side
　　A bold transgressor quivers.
Why shakes he so ?　Is he not strong ?
Effects to causes must belong.
The forest depths of gloom are still,
　　Nor tell they what they witness ;
But, oh, Agnoscens dreams of ill,
　　Yea, things which have no fitness ;
And, seeing with his spirit-eyes,
He from impending mischief flies.

———

Richard.　Margaret.　Carolus.　Voices.

RICHARD.

There was heard, it is true, what they called a voice.
It was naught but an infantile fear that choice
Was about to be made which should never be,
And that something would happen to you or me.
I am sick of the world for its constant blame,
And more sick of the Church for its cry of shame.
I'm ashamed that the nature which lives in all
Cannot have its full scope ; but the mind is small,
And when bandaged with doctrines can never thrive.
Let all parts of its action be kept alive.

For why are we put here if we may not live,
Nor the freedom that's wanted quite freely give ?
I am vexed, even maddened, and fain would paint
How much I suffer still through the creed's restraint.
The misguidance of home, and the Bible in school,
Have embittered my life, and I now am a fool.
If you call me rebellious, I scorn the charge,
But, the tether removed, I my range enlarge.

MARGARET.

Oh, Richard, be still, and control your ire ;
Your words are the sign of an inward fire ;
You burn yourself ; you may burn me too ;
The wrath you indulge must some mischief do.

RICHARD.

Not a little you vex me by what you now say ;
And I fear you will rue that you met me to-day.

MARGARET.

Why should I if you cool your mind ?
We then in talk some joy may find.
But I have now disturbing doubt
Touching the things you talk about.
Just learn to prize the good of life,
And soothe your mind, now torn with strife.

RICHARD.

I talk to you of things we know,
As on our pleasant path we go,
    And are you doubting still ?

The road is straight before our feet,
And when we here each other meet,
　Our rule is our own will.

A Voice.

Trees in beauty flourish here,
　Gracing all the seasons ;
Birds are flitting far and near,
　With or without reasons.
Soft the sward for weary feet ;
　No one here need falter ;
This the lovers' own retreat,
　Pathway to the altar.
Ye have come to please yourselves,
　No one you pursuing ;
Oh, forget not there are elves
　Set to watch wrong-doing.

Margaret.

What danger can for us be here ?
My frame is trembling as through fear.
But I of words must now be chary,
Or you will sneer and call me fairy.
Lucia, fearing things that shame,
Left us ere this way we came.

Richard.

What danger is there in this wood
For you ?　No chance of aught but good.
Carolus comes, our constant friend ;
Us he would from ourselves defend.

What comes he now to bid us do ?
Angry with me, he pities you.
Him I detest, but must control
The passion that upsets my soul.

I thought we had escaped his glance,
And found for this day better chance.
But we must meet him as a friend,
And quickly his obstruction end.

MARGARET.

Ere we withdrew an hour ago,
He said some words that made me know
   My life must change or be undone ;
And still I feel with pain that truth.
May we not mourn a ruined youth,
   Wrong boasting of a victory won !

CAROLUS.   [farm

We have gone through the wood and looked over the
Lying out far beyond the gate locked. What a charm
In the landscape !   Its beauty no words can express.
I was moved to go over ; the truth I confess ;
But I felt it my duty once more to seek you ;
And to urge you to ponder the course ye pursue.

RICHARD.

Who locked that gate ?   Why broke you not a way ?

CAROLUS.

I had no right, and more I need not say.

RICHARD.

My might shall give me right when I am there.

MARGARET.

O Richard, spare yourself this anger, spare.

CAROLUS.

But we do not agree in the views that we take
Of what must for a man his true happiness make.
While my friend's for lucidity, I am for light,
And while he is for sweetness, I'm simply for right ;
But the right of the gospel with sweetness combines,
And the light of that gospel for every one shines.
You might argue and wrangle till doomsday itself ;
Let the question be settled and laid on the shelf.

RICHARD.

Theology galls me, and I can not bear it ;
Why does it pursue me and drive me to dare it ?
Confounded be all who theology favour !
To me of insanity there is a savour
In all that they say.   But I will in sadness
Turn from them, disgusted, lest I sink to madness.

MARGARET.

Be sure your language is too strong ;
You seek excuse for something wrong.

RICHARD.

Oh, say not that.

MARGARET.

But I believe it true.
Claims not your conscience just the same of you ?

RICHARD.

If I am wrong, can you be right ?

MARGARET.

Alas, we sin against the light.

CAROLUS.

Yes, the way of transgressors in darkness must end,
In the gall wherewith sweetness none ever can blend.

RICHARD.

Transgression ? No.   Infirmity !
Confirmed the doctrine is, for me.
I will not this dispute prolong,
But read you Lucidus's song.
You may suppose it bears no sense,
But it will bring relief immense :—

Vice and virtue, right and wrong,
True and false, and weak and strong,
　　Are words or things :
When they are words their meanings change,
As culture's gamut, in its range,
　　Occasion brings ;
And words are trinkets for the clever ;
Worn out with use they will be never.

Right and virtue, vice and wrong,
Weak and false, and true and strong,
    Are things or words :
When they are things, their meanings glare ;
It needs no wit to know them there :
    How like the birds
That fill the air with ceaseless chatter,
And make one wonder what's the matter.

Vice and virtue, false and wrong,
Right and weak, and true and strong :
    Trinket and bird !
When things are settled they remain ;
But meanings changed may change again.
    So have I heard
That vice to virtue was uplifted,
And wrong set right seemed scarcely shifted.

A Voice.

'Tis the song of a singer who trifles with truth ;
When too late he will mourn for the ways of his youth ;
That his notions are false he can never perceive ;
Should you teach him the truth, he himself would
    deceive.
A poor victim of words ! Should you pity or scorn ?
Ah me, pity him, pity him, wretched, forlorn.
He is mastered by vocable elegance quite,
And is groping in darkness, but boasting of light.

Margaret.

What a wonder is such teaching !
Who is saved by culture-preaching ?

RICHARD.

I said you'd hear my views confirmed,
    And, Margaret, it is so.
Their sense into your mind is wormed ;
    And through the wood we go.

MARGARET.

How can I go ?   If I do wrong,
I shall interpret that light song.
We oft before have missed our way ;
I hoped for better luck to-day.

RICHARD.

What better is ?   I walk in light,
    Sweetness my rule ;
I see, desire, and claim my right ;
    We're not at school.
My friend, adieu ; your thoughts are bright,
    But I'm no fool.

MARGARET.

You want him not within your sight ;
    But do keep cool.
Richard, I live in constant fright ;
Why should I with my conscience fight,
And turn clear day to gloomy night ?

CAROLUS.

Once more they go, and I am left alone,
To pray and think, in pain too deep for words.

D

What have I seen where culture boasts and sings ?
The fabric of philosophy has sunk
In mire. Fair was it ere it fell, and some,
Amazed, deceived, looked on it and admired.
Who wondered most will wonder more to see
The promise unfulfilled, the beauty gone.
Light had been found if sought with earnest heart ;
But now the eye is dim that might have seen,
In truth's own sunshine, what is good for man.

 O dear deceit, philosophy, that cam'st
Proclaimed a clean and holy thing, thou art
Discredited, nor sweet, nor light, nor pure.
All virtues were to flourish in thy day,
And cries of woe on earth to die erelong,
As passeth night when morning paints the sky.
What meets us now ? The blasphemy of minds
Impure, whose thoughts are steeped in wantonness.
Vain is that creed, though true, which checks not sin ;
Vain is the boast of him who pampers self ;
And vain the light that leads not unto God,
That new philosophy which hides the truth.
And says a tree is good whose constant fruit
Is vice or wrong. O bold philosophers,
Know ye the harvest of the seed ye sow ?
Whither lead ye the trusting souls of men ?
Where has your doctrine filled a life with joy,
Where brought the calm of soberness and peace ?

 Within the sylvan shade blaspheming caught
My ear. It mingled with the strains of song,
Poured forth to win by witchery of words,

While truth was naught, or secondary deemed.
Can thoughts of minds untrue fit men to guard
A nation's honour ?   Can the heart impure
Teach youth to live ?   Let history reply,
Whose voice is thunder all can hear.   Where now
The empires once so great in arms, in song,
In art, in feats of skill ?   O'erwhelmed in vice,
In error, how they sank and died, prepared
As offering for their vengeful foes, the scourge
Of God Almighty, whom they had defied !
The spring of life grew foul, and poured a stream
Corrupt.   A while was licence sweet, but soon
The revels of iniquity turned sour.
They who had loved them once now hated more,
And sought in suicide their sole relief.
Godless in thought, in heart, in life, and worse
Becoming daily, they, too vile to be
Endured, were by the earth rejected.   Right
Eternal, God's own law, avenged in dire,
Yea, nameless punishments, drove them away,
And bade oblivion hide their rottenness.
The law of right abides and knows no change.
Divine authority can not be spurned
And unavenged remain.
                              O men, pursue
Your doctrine, and know how it spreads itself
Where ye have never gone, yea, where your books
Are still unread.   Man's flattered vanity
Is proud to be sustained by such as ye,
Whose names are symbols for the licence loved.

'Tis said ye think theology must die,
Since all the charities of Christ have grown
From stories false, and wonders never done,
And myths which genius found in fancy's field,
And knowledge must o'erturn the Testaments,
That man may freedom find where science rules.

    Have ye disclosed the mystery of life,
And drawn from nature the acknowledgment,
That ye need now no messenger divine,
To tell of God, of sin, of hell, of heaven ?
Ye pant for breath in your hot haste to know,
And, knowing, boast that yet ye can not tell ;
Then cease to lead the feeble soul from God.

    Lo, at your feet a steep which ye know well !
There some unwise advance, taught by yourselves
To try the easy road, which leads to depths
That ye have not explored, nor hope to tread.
Would lead the trustful to their endless bane ?
What the due recompense for such a feat ?
Will conscious merit be its own reward ?
O men, beware ; call back the youth who hastes
With ease and pleasure to Avernian deeps,
Nor knows the danger of the path he treads ;
Or, meet rebuke for having lured him down ;
And then at last, repenting, cry, Too late,
And drop yourselves where light will never shine,
Nor hope assuage the anguish of the soul,
While memory mocks the striving to forget.

A VOICE.

    Mark thou the inspirèd bard
    Whom conscience doth not guard,

When bid correct his false-toned lyre.
  He sees nor fault nor harm,
  Though aiming but to charm,
By cheat of words, for fame or hire.

  Mark thou the boasting sage
  Who calmly can engage,
With sophistries, receptive youth.
  Is it not work unwise
  To darken searching eyes,
And teach to seek, not find, the truth ?

  Mark thou the faithless guide
  Who takes dishonest pride
In points of dark impurity,
  Wherein he deftly darts
  Through unsuspecting hearts
What kills their sweet security.

  Mark thou the vagrant youth
  Who hates the curb of truth,
But loves to wear sin's heavy chain.
  For him there comes a day
  When he, in sore dismay,
Great loss will find for little gain.

  Mark thou the trusting child
  Who, when misled, beguiled,
Walks on where folly points the way.
  She surely will at last,
  Her maiden gladness past,
Have night that melts not into day.

And mark thou, mark thou, all
Who will not humbly call
On God for help in time of need.
Alas, for none of them,
Can any giant stem
The tide that rolls with whelming speed.

VI.—HOME.—(EVENING).

The rudest swain gives heed
When o'er the verdant mead
The song, let loose, of philomel
Makes rapture swell, and swell, and swell,
    Till none that hears the sound
    Can find, by thought profound,
In words, or shouts of loud acclaim,
Expression, sign, or worthy name,
    For such delight.
    The very night
Is grudged to sleep while such a strain
Doth its delicious thrall maintain
    O'er ear and mind.
    In town confined,
    Agnoscens dreams ;
    And to him seems
Restored on earth man's pristine joy ;
    For sweeter notes than philomel's
    Rise from the hearth where virtue dwells,
And works of love all hands employ.

Father.   Mother.   Sons.   Daughters.   Servant.

          ~~DAUGHTER.~~ Son

Sweet is the savour of the psalm
    We sang :this morn, as daily ;
And great the power the soul to calm
    Of writers such as Paley.

Their arguments the mind protect ;
   Right glad am I to know them ;
And I will not henceforth neglect,
   When duty is, to shew them.

~~Son~~:

We've read and read, to our own good ;
   I'm glad we ever did it ;
Else, wanting proofs, my faith had stood
   Perilled, when those who bid it
Shew forth its origin divine
   Demand of me a reason ;
Young sceptics think their talents shine
   When they to Christ do treason.

SECOND SON.

With power the holy scripture came
   To me, rebuking coldness,
And teaching I must speak the name
   Of Jesus Christ with boldness ;
And I will do it with my might,
   Though man's approval fail me ;
I'll wave this torch of heavenly light,
   If bitter words assail me.

SERVANT.

The children in this house are taught
   That pleasure walks with duty ;
The parents have true goodness sought
   As fairest form of beauty.

They run to work, as blithe as larks,
    Great pleasure in their faces.
O that I too may shew the marks
    Of all the Christian graces.

MOTHER.

We aim to direct them in paths that are pure,
    And wait on the Lord for the grace which we need ;
Ability is not life's strain to endure,
    Unless in the training the parents succeed
In binding the heart to the thing that is good,
And guiding the feet in a way understood.

We felt it was never too soon to begin ;
    Ere words had a meaning our spirit was felt.
The purpose their being completely to win
    In mind from the first has unceasingly dwelt.
That path they still love which their tiny feet trod ;
Through us they have learned their relation to God.

FATHER.

    To-day in town was told a tale
    Which made me bitterly bewail
    The miseries of misguided youth,
    Who lose their love for trust and truth.

    It made me wonder what would be,
    If I should e'er such sinning see
    In child of mine.   I fear that I,
    By sorrow slain, should mourning die.

    The boy was early sent to school,
    And learned of Christian life the rule ;

A while he walked with good intent,
And seemed on lawful living bent.

The parents said " The boy is strong,
Temptation will not lead him wrong ; "
And forth they sent him to the town,
Where honour should his labour crown.

There many days he did so well,
No words their honest joy could tell ;
Their hope must surely be fulfilled,
And every rising fear was stilled.

By tempters overcome, at length
He fell, nor felt the boasted strength ;
He chose to follow their foul choice
Who in impurity rejoice.

They lured him on to worse and worse ;
He drank, he swore, he stole a purse ;
Tried, guilty, he in prison lies,
And pure parental pleasure dies.

MOTHER.

I fear he never loved the light ;
Haply his heart was never right
With God ; and when temptation came
He fell as one already lame.
It is not safe to let a child,
However gentle, good, and mild,
Have much of that communication
Wherein for him is strong temptation.

SECOND SON.

In our street in the morning I talked with a boy
Who has wronged the good man that has found him
      employ ;
He has been reprimanded, but stays at his post,
Not the guilt but publicity troubling him most.
He has conscience, he told me, but thinks he should live
In the way which will him greatest happiness give.
So he laughs at the Bible and mocks at the creed,
And despises the things of which we have felt need.
As he early went forth from the guard of the home,
And decides for himself how and where he may roam,
I am pained as I think how he needs the protection
Of one having power to insist on correction.

FATHER.

From such a case we lessons learn.
Knows he what is man's chief concern ?
The lad will fail, ye may depend,
And run his course to no good end.
Be thankful, children, ye have been
Taught how to judge such things when seen.
We cannot wonder when a youth
Ne'er led to love and practise truth,
Goes wrong and casts restraints aside.
Great ill must such a one betide.

DAUGHTER.

We kept together as we went,
As when in childhood we were sent
    For health on sunny days.

Delighted with our perfect home,
We have no wish afar to roam,
   In new and doubtful ways.
But books, and art, and music here
Are full of joy through all the year.

SECOND DAUGHTER.

Yes, and we now must have a song,
For pleasures here to each belong,
And we in music go together
As when we walked by yonder heather.
Come, mother, choose what pleases you,
And both the boys will help us two.

MOTHER.

My sons must join their sisters.

SECOND SON.

Have we once failed to help them well ?
I doubt if in the town there dwell
   Such brotherly assisters.

SATAN.

Never since the birth of light
   Saw I what was more annoying ;
   Never in my fell destroying
Madder was my soul of might.

SON.

A lesson well I learned to-day,
   And shall not soon forget it.

Quickly I learned it on the way,
  And now in verse have set it.
The music chosen suits the sense,
  And we will join in singing.
God grant us purity's defence,
  The fruit of our upbringing :—

    " I sigh when I remember,
      That of my life's fleet year
    I'm in the drear December,
      And know the end is near."
    So said an aged sinner
      Whom I had seen before ;
    His face was growing thinner
      And marks of meaning bore.

    A neighbour saw his sorrow,
      A man as old as he,
    And said, " My friend, to-morrow,
      My years will eighty be.
    My end is drawing nearer,
      Few must my months now be ;
    But hope grows daily clearer
      I shall my Saviour see."

    The two gazed on each other,
      And silent stood a while ;
    One strove a sigh to smother,
      And sweetly one did smile.
    One face told me most clearly
      Of holy joys within ;
    The other told how nearly
      Had come the doom of sin.

With vision of those faces,
  I, musing, walked away.
The Christian's healthy graces,
  The worldling's woe-worn clay,
To me were meet confession
  How grace divine doth guard,
While pathways of transgression
  From first to last are hard.

MOTHER.

Conviction deepens in my mind
  Redoubled care is needed,
That we to God our being bind,
  Tempters and fools not heeded.
The song, the words, and all the scene
  Have taught me lessons, read between.
Dangers there are on every hand;
  More and yet more I feel it;
From such as form this happy band
  'Twere folly to conceal it.
Ye have been warned from early days,
And know to walk where safety stays.

SATAN.

Yes, they are warned, and I am thwarted;
  Parental care my nature hates;
  My hope to ruin those abates
Who are with such effect. exhorted.

FATHER.

Now let us read the sacred word,
Wherein the voice of God is heard,

And raise our song of glad thanksgiving,
And crave the grace of holy living :—

The Lord in whom we put our trust
Is merciful to all and just ;
His hand with bread supplies our board,
And he by us is loved, adored.
We hope, when perfected in grace,
To see with joy his glorious face.

The providence, which guards our ways
And fills with blessing all our days,
Is large and bountiful and kind,
Nor in our sorrow fails to find
Some cause of joy.   O Lord of all,
We at Thy footstool humbly fall.

May grace our erring feet restrain,
And comfort when our hearts complain,
Vouchsafed to us in full supply,
As forth we go new paths to try ;
Aided by thee from hour to hour,
We shall o'ercome the tempter's power.

We worship Thee, O glorious King,
Rejoicing now Thy praise to sing ;
Trusting in Thee, we fully rest,
And, in Thy smile supremely blessed,
We serve Thy gracious pleasure still,
And long to know Thy perfect will.

Watch o'er us through the shades of night,
That when we see the morning light,

We may again, (our strength renewed,)
With Thy sweet grace afresh endued,
In paths of duty onward go,
More and yet more of Thee to know.

On Thy unbounded mercy cast,
From day to day, while life shall last,
May we to all in words confess,
And in our joyfulness express,
The bliss of souls through Christ forgiven,
And live on earth in peace with heaven.

SATAN.

Such songs I utterly abhor ;
    They are the product of the light,
    And vex my soul and cause me fright.
How well I know what they are for.

MOTHER.

This day abundant food for thought
By observation has been brought
        Us all.
The blessing we from God receive,
The grace o'er others' woes to grieve,
Desire their burdens to relieve,
        Us call
To do at once our earnest part,
With ready mind and thankful heart.
May He who guides the faithful soul,
To well-meant effort deign control,

And grant that we may blessing bring,
To make the sorrow-stricken sing
For joy of heart. So shall we know
Angelic joys while here below.

FATHER.

I pity children whose unthinking friends
Restrain them not. Nor jealous care attends
The words and ways whence vice or virtue springs ;
Nor just authority correction brings
When passion, temper, or temptation sways
The course pursued, by choice, in plastic days.
Where Christ hath placed them children should be kept ;
Else better had it been if they had slept
The sleep of death in infancy.

MOTHER.

Why then
Is childhood left with such unthinking men ?

FATHER.

I pity babes who breathe a poisoned air
And have for future years no prospect fair
Of strength or health. May not their angels weep
At sight of them, and, as they vigil keep,
Wish they were safe within a purer sphere ?

MOTHER.

I pity maidens who, when they should fear,
Give confidence where it is not deserved.
How oft have such to darksome pathways swerved,

E

And mourned at length, repenting, but too late,
The bitterness of an avenging fate.

FATHER.

I pity all that walk in crooked ways
Of vice.   Soon pleasure palls, and then, the days
Of brightness ended, deepening glooms begin,
And conscience, tortured, is bound fast in sin.

MOTHER.

The path of pureness is the way of health.
There pleasure walks, with true and lasting wealth
Endowed.   The path of vice is short, and ends
In what none, knowing, for himself intends.
How can a man walk on with open eye,
Content to live, in order just to die ?
O children, be ye good, live pure, do right.
So shall ye walk to heaven, led in the light,
In meekness clothed, in Christ's own brightness bright.

FATHER.

True goodness comes, when sought, through love divine,
And he who always would in virtue shine
Must pray and wait for aid.   They teach a lie
Who labour to persuade men to rely
Upon themselves, nor sue for saving grace.
How can a sinner stand before the face
Of justice pure ?   They who from God's own truth
Would turn their fellow men are bound, forsooth,
To judge the fruit of what they sow.   The youth

Whose story I have told has drunk a cup
Prepared by error, and may drink it up.
What then can it do for him ?   All may see
In dark beginning what the end must be.
Shun ye all doubtful things, and go with men
Of faith and reason.   Ye shall prosper then,
Laborious live, and joyous die, for ever blessed.
With Him who errs not, leave ye all the rest.

VII.—A WAY-SIDE INN.

———

Agnoscens dreams that o'er and o'er
He walks upon the heathy moor,
   And wisdom learns from rustic child.
The simple finds the precious lore,
And treasures up, in ample store,
   The wealth of spirits undefiled.

———

Richard.   Margaret.   Lucidus.   Victor.   Blanda.

LUCIDUS.

The walk was pleasant in the vale ;
I wish we could at once prevail
   On all the town to try it.
The rich and poor are just alike ;
Masters oppress, and servants strike ;
   Improvement !   I deny it.

VICTOR.

Slow progress is the rule.   Better at length
   Will take the place of worse ; of that be sure.
In life's close contest victory goes with strength ;
   And feebleness declines, nor can endure.
The fittest will survive of men and things and habits,
The useless disappear, as foxes kill the rabbits.

LUCIDUS.

Foxes are few, but rabbits plentiful ;
  Bad similes need not obscure the truth.
To me your doctrine's trite. Still, dutiful,
  I will instruct and guide inquiring youth.
Letters give light, and literature in sweetness
Has no compeer ; doctrines I teach of meetness.
     Why come not townsfolk on the way
     We travelled in the vale to-day ?
     Fitness for them would be, in weather
     Like this, to scent the breezy heather.

VICTOR.

Nature is wonderful. The more I see
  The more am I amazed. The smallest things
Are great in teaching ; and it seems to me
  The greatest want of peasants and of kings
Is knowledge of the world wherein they live.
That knowledge I to all would gladly give.

LUCIDUS.

And letters too are wonderful. The more
  I know, and read, and write in proper form,
The more am I confounded and dismayed
  At the Philistine dulness of the age.
  The graceful song, the lucid printed page,
Wherein is thought with art of style conveyed,
  However much the dull divines may storm,
Open for man to his true good the door.
Culture must check the vices of the race,
And man for life and work right firmly brace.

SATAN.

What matters it if thought is quite untrue ?
   I value books as they can lead astray
   The mind of youth ; I am in no dismay.
With such strong help fresh mischief I can brew.
Science and art, when godless and profane,
   And letters, when the aim is but to please,
   Are strong enough to serve my cause ; and these,
If loss to others, are to me great gain.
Why need I toil when others do my work ?
I'll be content to tempt, and watch, and lurk.

RICHARD.

   Our bard has gone with his great friend.

MARGARET.

Chance may for us companions send.
A pleasure party passed this way,
And will return ere dies the day.

RICHARD.

His doctrine's good ; I like it well,
And to you, Margaret, often tell
   How aptly serves my sense of right.
Culture and science I admire,
But I am governed by desire
   To take, and hold with conscious might,
What some would say I cannot claim.
I know they think my life a shame
   And fiercely censure my delight.

MARGARET.

What is the culture you admire ?
Where is it when your strong desire,
   O'erpowering reason, drives you mad,
And leaves you helpless on the floor ?
I tell you now, as oft before,
   The drunkard's end is very sad.
You drew me down, and draw me still,
Submissive to your boundless will,
   As if I no true freedom knew.
Leave you I must except you mend ;
Bnt if you will your errors end,
   My joy for you I shall renew.

RICHARD.

Am I a drunkard then ?

MARGARET.

         You're what you are,
And I must suffer with you, as I know.

RICHARD.

Oh, you are very good ; you are the star
   To guide my life which else would end in woe.

MARGARET.

To guide your life ? Ah me ! You say you find
   In teachers of the day whose books you read
Directive aid. How can a woman's mind
   Guide you aright ? Like you, I guidance need.

Not now again will I the tale unwind.
Take heed lest culture your weak conscience smother.

RICHARD.

Are they not right who tell us we are here
To please ourselves ? You know I do no other

MARGARET.

The boasting talk wherein you mock and jeer
Has grown from things not taught you by your
mother.
You know the way but do not walk therein.

RICHARD.

And there's no curse that will avenge my sin.
Of that I am most sure.

MARGARET.

Be not so certain.
Things are not hidden by the thickest curtain.
A silent stranger hears this our contention,
And may be worse for having heard us mention
Such subjects here. What think you, gentle stranger,
Of what we said ? You look like one in danger !

BLANDA.

Ere my friends went on their walk
I was hearing great men talk.
They and you have taken away
All the charm of life to-day.

MARGARET.

What is culture to the fool
Who knows not himself to rule ?

RICHARD.

I am cool, but you are hot ;
Here and now rebuke me not.
Let us hear what may be said
By this maiden, o'er whose head
Few the summers that have flown.
Little sorrow hath she known.
I admire her rustic beauty.

MARGARET.

She may teach us both our duty.

BLANDA.

They declaimed against the preachers,
And would have us follow teachers
Who deny to Christ the right
To be held the world's great Light.
What can young ones do without Him ?
O. that I knew more about Him.

RICHARD.

She is simple as nature and wise as a sage ;
Her simplicity hurts while her manners engage.

MARGARET.

And she a rebuke hath to both of us brought ;
I am vexed that I asked her to tell us her thought.

BLANDA.

But I know the power of sin.
Satan still doth conquest win
Over those whom error leads.
Victory his malice feeds.
They have qualms of conscience known
Who to callousness have grown.
Mournful when the feelings cease
Which should steadily increase.
This I see in godless youth
Who forsake the way of truth,
And their sensibility
Kill by fruitless vanity.
Such may seek but cannot find
What contents or heart or mind.
Evermore on pleasure bent,
Why should they themselves torment ?
Their example is to me
Saddest of the things I see.

MARGARET.

Already you have said enough ; and when
    I want a sermon I will go to church.
Women I cannot bear in place of men ;
    For less than you have said some get a birch.

BLANDA.

I must withdraw to meet my friends,
And, as our conversation ends,
Permit me just a word to say

Of what has troubled me to-day.
The great men talked and talked at length
Like giants wrestling with their strength;
But what they said appeared to me
To lack the sweetness, melody,
And power to comfort, of that truth
Which I have known through all my youth.
Ye are disciples of the wise,
And walk in ways which please your eyes.
I fear ye seek but have not found,
For your desires, the solid ground
 Of right and reason.   Do ye see ?

MARGARET.

A maid so bold to teach as she
I have not met since I was born.
Oh, how she blows her little horn.

RICHARD.

Sorry I am we thus begin
To talk to strangers at an inn.
We little reckoned we should find
Such hectoring if we spoke our mind.

BLANDA.

The truth offends them, and their anger proves
 Them not content.   Spoke I the first to them
Or they to me ?   Their anger but removes
 Far off the hope that what they needs condemn
They will forsake.   The soul has wants, I know,

Which doctrines such as they have uttered here
Assuage not but embitter.   I will go
   And weep for them.   I tremble as I fear
The doom which them awaits, a sad condition,
A woe foretold, relieved by no contrition.

RICHARD.

What meant it when she asked if we could see ?

MARGARET.

What could she mean but to rebuke both me
And you ?   Perhaps she found in what we said
Suspicion we by teachers have been led
Astray, where darkness gathers o'er the eyes
Of vapouring fools who think themselves too wise
To heed the parsons ; and she may be right.
What but destruction then have we in sight ?
What, if her judgment should prove just, and we
Good not on earth, nor anywhere, should see ?

RICHARD.

I hate restraint on arm or mind.
   I ought to know what's best for me ;
   And, Margaret, I must still be free ;
Henceforth my will no one shall bind.

MARGARET.

And I must take my lot with you.
   Sages as guides should bring content ;
   But I confess I never meant
To embark with your sagacious crew.

RICHARD.

How life has changed since we began :
  I hate the counsels of my youth,
    Though once I took them for the truth ;
And freedom hath made me a man.

SATAN.

They do the work for me. My business thrives
  On falsehood, anger, hatred, wilfulness,
    And misbelief. They nothing gain, 'tis true,
Who close their eyes to God's own truth. He strives
  In vain and fails who seeks his happiness
    Where bones of those who fell in folly strew
The plain. I laugh at them, wond'ring they know
  It not. Fools are they and naught else. I grin,
    The ghost of pleasure flitting o'er my pain,
As I foresee the fruit which those who sow
  Such seed must reap. Harvests at length begin,
    And comes the end, with most tremendous rain
Of tribulation, measured out to all.
The souls of men before Jehovah fall !

Yet will not all be blessed. Laughing I mock,
  And jeering taunt my dupes. I do the same
    Again and yet again in every age.
What matters it to them if judgments shock
  The common mind and gentler sinners tame ?
    Those whom I cheat but curse the more and rage.
It matters naught to me, if my designs
  Succeed. Teachers and guides of youth, whose books,
    Informed by genius, lead the inquirer down

To atheistic depths, where gloom confines
    The soul, and whence no one with hopeful looks
        Can gaze on high, receive the righteous frown
Of those who love mankind.   But I love none ;
My nature burns, with enmity undone.   ·

'Tis my sole joy to see my dupes betrayed.   [safe ;
    Strong have they thought themselves and wise and
        But, lo, a girl has doctrine meekly taught
Which rankles in their breasts.   She but conveyed
    Thoughts true and wholesome; yet, Oh, how they chafe
        Rebellious minds, that are true bond-slaves, caught
And held by me, but by themselves accursed !
    I shake my sides with laughter as I see
        The madness.   This my plan succeeds.   I wait
To see its end.   As one who long has nursed
    A feeble life and wondered what would be
        Its issue, I man's evil fostered.   Late
I saw it spring to vigorous life ; and how
Dance I and boast to see it spreading now !

Men help me well.   In guise of truth, they stand
    To beckon on their fellows in the way,
        And promise pleasure, freedom, ease.   How vain
The weening !   They have broken the command
    Of Heaven in teaching falsehood.   What they say
        Is turned to deeds ; and why should men restrain
Propension, if no one has right to bid
    Them stop ?   I wish them not to cease.   They serve
        Themselves and me ; and we together build

A monument for worlds to study. Did
  They know the madness, 'twould at once unnerve
    Their arm, and they would fail, their spirits filled
With uttermost dismay, to do my work.
I goad them on, and in concealment lurk.

Away they speed
In very greed
  Of sin ;
Nor to restrain
Themselves for pain
  Begin.
I watch them well,
On earth in hell
  And shame.
  To name
The deeds they do
And sure will rue,
Is not my plan,
Since thus I can
  But fail.
I must and will
Over them still
  Prevail.
Let pleasure smile
And sin beguile,
  That I
May reach the end
To which I tend,
  Nor sigh

To see at last
All hoping past
　　For them
Whom their own lives,
While thought survives,
　　Condemn.
On, on they press !
Oh, the madness !
　　My soul
Shall scorn their ways
When no more days
　　Shall roll.

VIII.—A COUNTRY MANSION.

Agnoscens sees, while yet he dreams,
A thunderbolt, which to him seems
   Sent to confound
A soul that trembles on a brink,
'O'er which to ruin one may sink,
   If careless found.

Lucidus. Victor. Aretas. Dardan. Phane. Hermes.
Regnans. Probus. Optatus.

OPTATUS.

Sad news has come from town to-day
   Of Richard, once our pride ;
In angry talk one heard him say
   He could not life abide,
And pitied him. He missed his way,
   And now is glad to hide.

PROBUS.

A friend who knows him well has said
That ever since the books he read
Of some bold men, his life has been
One ceaseless effort, hot and keen,
   To find enjoyment ;

And now the doctrine to present
In practice, with entire consent,
  Is his employment.
But how he lives and where he goes,
No one among us surely knows;
But, Oh, my pity for him grows.

REGNANS.

What pleasure seeks he that he should not seek ?

PROBUS.

He boasted he had cast off all restraint
Of creed and doctrine, and poured out complaint
Against his friends, no blush upon his cheek.

REGNANS.

What means this loud and wild destructive stir,
  Raised by the thinkers ?   What are they about,
  That men of lives corrupt their names can shout ?

OPTATUS.

Perhaps they proudly think they good confer.
  In that let us take leave to doubt the claim.
  If they have ruined Richard, what but shame
Belongs to them ?   My judgment I defer.

PROBUS.

Let us weigh facts and their true meaning see ;
  And let us join, with what we think, the thought
  Of scientific men, together brought
For social pleasure.   They will help us three.

OPTATUS.

They come, and we will tell them our sad news ;

REGNANS.

And soon elicit their peculiar views.
We of their works have partial study made,
But Richard boasts that he has them obeyed.
Know they this fact ? Will they, think ye, confess
The new philosophy creates distress ?
They come ; I bid them welcome in your name,
Proud to converse with men of honest fame.
We welcome you, sage counsel needed here.

PROBUS.

The times are dark ; life's riddles now appear
Insoluble.   .

ARETAS.

     Humanity must rise,
Whate'er betide.   This is the truth, we know.

VICTOR.

The teeming earth and the resplendent skies
    Are growths of nature.

ARETAS.

         Here, for man, below
The stars, stands one true home. He lives and dies,
    And answers the great end with progress slow.

VICTOR.

The very worms are beautiful.   The earth
  Teems with instruction everywhere.   Behold
  Its mystic dance of life.   It must enfold
Deep potency which struggled into birth.

ARETAS.

Supreme on earth is man; my mind adores
The race that conquers all.

VICTOR.

     Mine but deplores
  The miseries of man ; I'm not so bold
As to suppose his doings have much worth.
Creation none has proved.   All things have grown.
  How they began to grow I do not see ;
  Such knowledge is too wonderful for me.
Development has now been clearly shown ;
But, to adore what yesterday began,
  Exceeds my reason ; and I stand amazed
At what I see from England to Japan.
Men worship still ; but in these boastful times
  How are they wiser than when first they gazed
Upon the spangled heavens and worshipped All ?
  My science has denied to me what some
Believe ; but they who worship man have reached
A wide extreme in Christian lands.   In climes
  Less favoured, man has been less falsely praised.
In deepest reverence I, convinced, will fall
  Before One Great Supreme.   The time will come
When in all lands true science must be preached.

HERMES.

Which science ?   Social laws direct affairs,
  And man's not master of himself.   I see
  It now.   Look o'er the sward at yonder tree.
What is the fruit its nature yearly bears ?
Who can that nature change ?   Not one.   So man
  But yields what grows, and can yield nothing more.
Our work is, all the facts of life to scan,
  Augment the vast accumulated lore
Of ages, and prune where an error grows.
Knowledge is life ; man lives but as he knows.
  Beyond my depth I ne'er have stepped,
  Ne'er o'er unsolvèd riddles slept.
  Strong are my books, which if ye read,
  For other teachers little need
  Will you disturb.   When men go wrong,
  It is because temptation's strong ;
  And I would teach and warn my friend
  By shewing him life's proper end ;
  And I would give to one and all,
  The old, the young, the great, the small,
  The knowledge of those social laws
  Whereby man all his treasure draws.

REGNANS.

Richard, 'tis pain to know, has turned aside.
  He boasts that he can fully justify,
  Though I should deeply mourn to hear him try,
His known divergencies, however wide.

LUCIDUS.

How runs his life ?   Has he abandoned letters,
  Books his companions once ? He knows them well,
  And in his mind, through aid of culture, dwell
Conspicuous powers which should be kept from fetters.

HERMES.

But has he read our books, and does he know
  Our systems ?

ARETAS.

        And, in chief, has he e'er felt
The dignity of manhood ?

OPTATUS.

           Ah, I smelt
His curse, and read his face ; he, as a crow
  Fares well on carrion, talked of things corrupt.

LUCIDUS.

You shock me much.

OPTATUS.

        And I was shocked myself,
  And spoke to him in manner too abrupt,
Asking him what outrageous peevish elf,
  To change his life and culture interrupt,
Had dared to come.

HERMES. '

Give social laws their due.
The man has fallen. There must be a few
Among the elect of science such as he.
Some may be shocked, but no such thing shocks me.

ARETAS.

Humanity is in him still, and we
    Must raise him and teach self-control, and shew
    His yielding mind where he goes wrong. He needs
No other teaching.

REGNANS.

Well, I clearly see
    He has your teaching, and must surely know
    All it can tell him ; but some noxious weeds
Have choked the plant of culture, and it droops.
His knowledge he holds at command, and still
    Of sociology, humanity,
    And culture talks, and boasts of liberty,
But nothing says of curbing his wild will,
    Which bears him off, as when an eagle swoops
    A helpless child away, or, amidst troops
On foot, a man must march, his place to fill.

LUCIDUS.

How he has thrown away his power ! It pains
    My mind most deeply.   Light and sweetness save
    From degradation.   Cruel as the grave·
Is such a fall ; it our fair record stains.

ARETAS.

The light begins to shine where culture dwells,
And true humanity on all things tells.

VICTOR.

Development will cease not, but is slow.

HERMES.

We gather facts, and erelong we shall know.

PHANE.

What will ye know that is unknown to-day ?
  Your pupil boasts of his discipleship,
And bears his learning down the way of vice.
Who'd have philosophy at such a price ?
  For your own shoulders he has twined a whip.
Where is the remedy ? Ye sages, say.
Unless ye can, by your sweet means, restore
  This erring pupil, who boasts of content
  To follow you, on his own vices bent,
Take my advice, and boast ye never more.

PROBUS.

The things alarm which we have heard to-day;
It is my joy that I have learned to pray.

LUCIDUS.

True beauty is a virtue of the mind ;
  All might through culture to perfection rise ;

The light of letters shines for men of eyes ;
And sweetness is the savour of the wise.

OPTATUS.

But where can we to-day true wisdom find ?
    One talks of facts, but boasts he cannot know,
And labours still to be a guide of men,
    Claiming the rights of leadership. I vow
He's not consistent ; for, except the mind
    Can know, what worth in facts discerned ? Below
Lie causes that elude the searching ken
    Most keen, most deep. Another wonders how
It came to pass that all of human kind,
    In simple ages of the world, could bow
In prayer to the Invisible ; and man,
    Weak man, he deems the only worshipful
E'er known. This race, to him, is one great whole
    Are all its parts to be alike adored ?
Who then, reason still left him, aught else can
    Believe than this new creed is fanciful ?
Another thinks that letters can control
    Unruly passion. Well, Richard restored
Might give of that some worthy evidence.
Restore him, or, for me, take learning hence ;
My boast shall be of what heals such a soul.

DARDAN.

There's no truth in the world whereon I can depend
    In these matters of faith ;
In the Church there's no error for which I contend,
    Whate'er Anti-church saith.

We have heard of the wonders theology works
    When philosophy fails ;
But we know that in all things a mystery lurks,
    And that nothing avails
To remove it.   Yet when, in the agony born
    Of suspense and dismay,
Men return to the Church that is true, and in scorn
    Of each new-fangled way,
Put their trust in that Church, and its doctrines receive,
    They are raised into might.
'Tis the privilege granted to those who believe,
    That they walk in the light.
If your friend had but known where the lustre of truth
    May for ever be seen,   [sooth,
He had sprung from the depths of his fall ; and, for-
    Had enlightenèd been.
Even now he must hie to the friend of the poor,
    The infallible Church ;
Else he soon will be lower and worse than before,
    And be left in the lurch.
It is clear he has gone in the way of the fool,
    And is doing so still,
As the truant runs off from the duties of school
    At the call of his will.
Let him hearken to me and to those who have found,
    In the doctrines I teach,
Ample counsel, direct, and sufficient, and sound.
    My perfection to reach
I have tried the philosophy, science, and art
    Of the great of the day ;

But by them I no more am induced to depart
   From the old certain way.   ·   [requires.
Those who doubt this may do what their conscience
But, remember how Richard with pity inspires.

HERMES.

This takes us back to days of superstition.

ARETAS.

'Tis the old threat of merciless perdition.

LUCIDUS.

Who by one deed would private judgment kill
Find it hard work their dogma to instil.
They would persuade to think tradition sound,
That it might friends enslave and foes confound ;
But men set free by culture know full well
No longer needed this old threat of hell.
No more we want that theologic thrall
Which through the ages held both great and small.
He who may think but as the Church requires
Can never gain the height to which aspires
The man of letters, in whom shines for all
A wit that sweetness brings from very gall ;
Whereas the truth itself yields bitterness
To men who dare not their own thoughts confess.
The direst foes of man within him dwell ;
Be cultured, Protestant, and all expel.

PHANE.

   Where fools are guides and children kings, .
      Disaster spreads ;

The creed which blind prescription brings
    Is for soft heads.
Your science and philosophy
    Are not for me ;
Tradition I will never try
    While I can see.
Richard's sad case a lesson teaches,
And to the thinker soundly preaches.

REGNANS.

These teachers never can agree ;
Yet stable truth must somewhere be.

OPTATUS.

I wish we then at once could find it,
And to our hearts for ever bind it.

PROBUS.

We have it in the words which fell
From Him who deigned on earth to dwell
A man of griefs, to sorrow born.
None that are wise His doctrines scorn.

ARETAS.

Good slowly comes as evil goes ;
Man can o'ercome his strongest foes ;
In his deep nature's convolution
Provision is for evolution ;
And what we see not men will see :
This truth is learned by heeding me.

Humanitarianism is strong ;
All virtues must to it belong.
The smirch which Richard gives the truth
A warning reads to earnest youth ;
But it will not make less the grace
That shines upon the very face
Of that fair system which I preach,
Desiring truth to all to teach.

SATAN.

Teach truth indeed! 'Tis windy promise all.
Were I not Satan, I on them should call
To see themselves as they are seen by me ;
But all I do must with my aim agree ;
And I must act, but be nor seen nor heard.
The course of Richard hath their spirits stirred ;
Before its end they will be more perplexed.
I doubt if they are serious ; they have vexed
Themselves, in vain attempts to find a way,
Like one who gropes in blindness, while the day
Enlightens all that see. They do my work,
Yea, do it well. Meanwhile I slily lurk
Beside them, and impose my soft deceits.
As one who on the highway strangers meets,
And tells them lies, and sends their feet astray,
So have I led them on from day to day.
Their doctrines please me much, their pupils more.
God is denied, and naught will now restore,
I think, the dogma cast away. It fires
My soul to see mere youths, whom faith inspires,

Confound the sages; but I trust erelong,
By doctrine false, loose thinking, ribald song,
And sights impure, to bring them round.   Ah, when
The end is gained, they'll serve me well, and then
A master they shall have whose subtle ways
Are watched with care by Him who all surveys.
Write on, ye sages, and, ye Richards, drink,
Nor ever once of your dark future think,
While on ye go to curse and be accursed;
It gives me joy to see you do your worst.
My laughter's madness; this I know too well;
My work destruction, and my home this hell,
Wherein my powers are steeped in bitterness
Which now to you who hear not I confess.
My hell is with me, in me, of me here,
And where I seek my ends in any sphere.
I live devoted to one steady aim
Wherein as valiant helpers you I claim.
Ride on in strength; I prize your growing power,
And will not warn you of the fatal hour,
When vengeance, long delayed, shall burst at last,
And ye impenitent be headlong cast,
To wonder, where no man will feed your pride,
Or from the truth your eyes one moment hide,
While such as strove on earth the soul to feed
With your dry husks shall starve in deepest need.

IX.—WESTMINSTER ABBEY.

[CHRISTMAS.]

As one, who muses near a brook
    Which ever purls
    But never whirls
The pebble from its cozy nook,
    A meaning brings
    For that which sings ;
    So men hear sound
    Of thought profound,
    And each explains,
    With care and pains,
    What he has heard,
    Howe'er absurd
The gloss he gives the words may be.
Why doth not each the fixed truth see ?
    Agnoscens dreams
    Of diverse schemes
    Which men contrive,
    To keep alive
Religion's form without its power.
    Where Jacob's stone
    Hath long been known,
He dreams he spends a reverent hour,
    And hears one preach
    Who much can teach,
Whose thoughts on wings celestial tower.
Around him crowd self-pleasing minds,

What sign that one in fifty finds
          The true sense meant
          By Him who sent
          In unsought grace,
          For all'our race,
The hidden wisdom of the skies,
Disclosed to meekness-opened eyes ?

———

*Hermes.   Aretas.   Lucidus.   Phane.   Regnans.   Lucia.
Margaret.   A Preacher.   A Choir.   A Crowd.*

ARETAS.

This is a sacred place, and this the time
Of solemn worship.   We may think, but need
Not speak.   In every nook of this grand pile
I see my views confirmed.   Mau's glorious power
Is here displayed.   To each great name is given
The meed of honour ; and we here may think
To our great profiting.   Oh, great, supreme
Is manhood !   Bards enjoy a deathless fame,
True immortality, within their own
Most sacred precinct.   Orators, and men
Of letters, statesmen, and creators bold
In art and science, with evangelists,
Explorers of the seas and continents,
And men of arms, and rulers of the Church,
The nation's worship share.   Humanity
Is great, divine, adorable ; and man
I worship ; and my nation worships man,
Though some may think they sing to One Great Cause.

Else why this temple given our rarest men ?
I would to all interpret what I see.
The day is dawning, and my views must spread.

LUCIDUS.

The thought of ages is embodied here ;
And this old fane is one great parable ;
But the Philistine crowds are unaware,
And daily pass without a worthy thought.
O that they knew where shines the light of mind,
And saw the moral beauty here displayed.
I come to think, within these walls, of fame,
Made sure to greatness by the right of work.
I toil, and taste to-day the sweets which draw
Me on.   Might I inscribe a worthy name
Upon the scroll which here endures, Ah, then
No words would tell the rapture I should feel.
The prayers are long, and sermons weary me,
But through this service I will wait and think.
Perchance my sympathetic soul will meet
Congenial themes and tremblingly respond
In forms which men will honour and preserve.
This is a house to teach the cultured mind,
Since here the thought of ages lives in stone.

HERMES.

Worship of images their law forbids,
Yet in this fane we see them everywhere.
Hither my mother led me when a child,
And I impressions bear of things I saw ;

G

But little stays with me of what I heard.
Ah, now have gone my early thoughts of life,
Of worship, and of man.   Our ancestors
Lived in the dark ; but slowly we emerge
To light, to worship ghosts no more.   We serve
The Great Unknown whose representatives
This house with honour crowns. Some forms are seen
In this great fane by right of worth supreme,
And tell to all who were the kings of men.
But some more honour have than was their due,
Since flattery decked their graves, dug here with gold ;
And other men more worthy sleep elsewhere,
Nor have the due memorial of their lives.
Honour will come at length to those who serve
Mankind.   Let us have facts, that we may judge
Of service and of worth.   This Christmastide
Brings back with pain thoughts of my early days.
Oh, could I worship as I worshipped then !
The power was lost before my mother slept,
And much I troubled her devoutest soul.
I wonder how she thought of me in death.
The hope were welcome we might meet again.
But who for me can bring to life dead creeds ?
How sweet was once the thought of heaven, the rest
Of saints ; but now my highest hope lives here,
Where immortality enshrines our kings.

PHANE.

Lo, the philosophers !   Why come they here ?
This is a Christian church.   From day to day

Is here confessed the creed, and prayers are said,
In confidence that God will hear them all.
In church, Humanitarian views no place
Can have, sweetness and light mean Christian truth,
And facts of life take their significance
From holy writ. But these philosophers
Have felt the human touch of Christmastide, ·
And here confess the power of Jesus Christ.
How it would please me now to know their minds,
But we must keep a reverent silence here.
The meaning of this meeting will be told,
And I shall find my present thoughts confirmed,
For I have laboured long to know my friends,
And to define their inharmonious views.

THE CHOIR.

Hail, Son of God ; we worship Thee,
   The child of Mary made,
And see with awe Thy majesty
   In meanest cradle laid.

We can not, Lord, forget the stall
   Which was Thy first abode,
But now, as there, before Thee fall,
   To chant our reverent ode.

With weary feet Thou trod'st the earth,
   To care and toil inured,
Didst bear our sorrows from Thy birth,
   By death hast life procured.

The love which made Thee thus, below,
 The servant of our race,
A secret is which those who know,
 With joy thy will embrace.

LUCIA.

A holy place; and holy men of God
Here lead us in our prayers. But, Ah, I see
Whom I have looked not for. God bless them all !

ONE OF THE CROWD.

They press me much; I wish I had not come.

MARGARET.

Yes, she is here. We parted near the wood.
I have not seen her since. Oh, had I gone,
As she that day, refusing to be led
By promise fair which yielded naught but harm,
I had come hither, as she comes to-day,
In health, with beaming face and conscience clear.
We parted then, our diverse ways to take.
I can not bear to gaze into her eye ;
Nor can I wish that she may see my face.

REGNANS.

My quiet home had been to me more sweet
To-day than London ; but this sacred place
Is compensation ; and the Christmas feast
Served here brings nourishment for needy souls.
Music becomes the season, and, for me,

The pealing organ lifts the heart to God.
O Lord, may I in spirit worship Thee,
And may Thy truth my hungry nature feed,
Descend Thy manna for this waiting crowd,
And be the meaning of the day disclosed.

HERMES.

The cleric voice, the pulpit tone, attuned
And tuned again, to let the nature out.

ARETAS.

'Tis true that we have sinned and gone astray
Like wand'ring sheep, but we against ourselves
Have sinned.   Humanity is great, divine !
Our thoughts, through such confessions, go astray,
Misled.   I would revise these ancient prayers,
Which grate on ears refined and mean too much.

THE CHOIR.

True, it is a matchless story,
    Oft with joy repeated here :
The incarnate Lord of glory
    Did in infant form appear.

When he came angelic gladness
    Made of sheepfolds holy ground,
Giving joy for fear and sadness
    To the lowly, duteous found.

We have heard the angels singing,
    (Nations listening on this day,)

And, our gladsome homage bringing,
   Chant with them the peaceful lay.

May we do what he approveth
   Who in yonder manger lies ;
Vanity his lot reproveth,
   Pride before His cradle dies.

LUCIDUS.

This music, sweetened science, pleases me.
I wish the crowd around me could enjoy,
As I, these forms refined. True culture here.
O that Philistines could behold such light
As shines for men of eyes throughout this fane.
I pity those who see not what I see,
And find no meaning in these Christian words,
Which tell of Him who brought the sweetest light.

PHANE.

For me no pleasure comes with Christmastide ;
But I must wait and bear the tedious rôle.
My sceptic soul resents authority.
What then, to me, can mean this festal day ?

REGNANS.

Welcome the wondrous story still. He came
To seek and save the lost and was despised.
O that mankind but knew that saving grace
Which fills the joyous life with love and peace.
This service is, to me, like fresh'ning dew.

LUCIA.

To me these prayers come as to thirsty lips
The stream. Glows my glad heart with thankfulness.
I love the Lord because He first loved me,
Sought out and found me as a wand'ring sheep,
And brought me home. O were He known to all!

MARGARET.

Where is my Christmas joy? Some thief has come
And stolen it. I wish I were not here.
These touching words, the music, and my thoughts
Undo me quite. How can I sing these hymns?
I might have saved myself this wretched hour.

LUCIDUS.

The grace of words yet serves the Christian Church.

REGNANS.

O that all knew the joy of loving Christ.

MARGARET.

Unlike these Christmas hymns to what at home
My mother sang with me when I, a child,
Drank in the wondrous tale now brought to mind.
Why came I in to be so much disturbed?

HERMES.

O mystic power of words! This ancient tale
Hath charmed the infant mind from age to age.
Once it charmed me, but cannot do so now.

The superstitions of my youth are dead,
And I against their like am vigilant.
Deceptive fancies shall not me control,
But still I yield when Christmas songs resound.

ARETAS.

Greatest of men ! before Thy majesty
I bow my head.   Humanity is great,
Divine !   This service proves my views correct.
It savours most of man's almightiness.
The race needs leaders still.   Can I be one ?

THE CHOIR.

Forgive, O Lord, our foolish pride,
　To Thy poor cradle brought ;
And by Thy lowly meekness chide
.　Our vain self-pleasing thought.

No want, no sorrow, didst Thou spurn
　That came to Thee for aid ;
This lesson from Thy lot we learn,
　On us the duty laid,

To hear the cry of helpless grief,
　To give of our best store,
That sorrow may have swift relief,
　And want may leave the poor.

PHANE.

They are not teachable.   I wish I were ;
But criticism has fenced my nature round,

And here I sit, nothing to learn at all.
It was not so when I came here a child.
We find to-day what we have eyes to see,
And all the blind must grope in broadest day.

LUCIDUS.

The sermon next ; what will the preacher do ?
All know I well before the text is read ;
Yea, I could preach, as preached the man whose name
I bear, to many dear for service done
And worth which all confess.   But other means
Have spread my thoughts afar ; and I have said
In books what some have thought but durst not tell.
I am a brother preacher in my way.

LUCIA.

The Lord will hear the prayer and bless us all,
While from the preacher's lips flow tender words
To win our hearts to do as we have sung.

LUCIDUS.

Once he stood on mount Calvary to preach,
Pouring his aptest thought on royal ears.
O had I heard him pass the Crucified !
Over his books weak piety hath wrung
Her hands.   I love the sight, in craft of words
A brother born, and honoured by his pen.
When he expounds the theme of Christmas, who
The legend can resist ?   His learned breath
Will move this crowd.   So waves the standing corn

When zephyrs breathe.　I will attend his words,
Watching the sparkles of that beauteous light,
Sweet and refreshing, of keen intellect,
Which naught but letters on this earth can give.

THE PREACHER.

Brethren beloved, that story has been heard
Which groweth old, but is for ever new.
What means this festival of ancient date ?
The Son of God, whose birth the day recalls,
Came forth to manifest eternal love
For man, o'erwhelmed in sin and desperate,
And to destroy the devil's works.　This now
My peerless theme.　It speaks that truth which men
All need, that they may know their being's weal
In God's design.　O could the message sound
In every ear through all the climes of earth !
In pagan lands the evil spirit reigns
A tyrant-king.　In cruelty and wrong,
In shameless ministries, in deeds of vice
We dare not name, his will despotic works ;
Nor in these Christian realms that will unserved.
Mark ye the fell design to sweep away
Beauty with peace and love.　Where he is king,
Bloom falsehood, hate, and war, and want. The youth
Who pleases him is smit with deep disease,
Wherein decays all loveliness.　The home,
If he commands, grows drear and desolate,
Whate'er of beauty, learning, grace, or art
The hearth adorns ; husband with wife contends,

Child mocking child with envious sneer,
While virtue, tortured, sinks and dies.   Alas,
Society is mourning ; for, in all
Its grades, are mothers weeping o'er the lost,
In innocence betrayed, and taught to sin.
Many the guards which should our youth protect,
Needed in school and college, as at home ;
For Satan yet holds active agency.
If seats of.learning are the homes of shame,
It is because he works in wantonness,
Puffs up the proud with lies, confounds the weak
With sophistries obscure, and puts an end,
By blasphemy, to prayer.   Ah, then he more
And more corrupts the vicious, while the truth
Is quite concealed with doubts and glosses false.
Happy the faithful few who watch his wiles,
Arming themselves with Christian panoply,
That they in fullest strength may serve the Lord.
    Satan has cursed our trade with selfishness ;
And greed, his liege, sits tyrant of the mart,
To smile or frown as he may most defraud.
Skill he perverts to teach immodesty,
Making of art a ministry of vice,
Distilling poison-nectar from the sink,
And luring innocence to taste and die.
The press, when he presides, of infamy
The servant is ; the simple it ensnares,
And vexes righteous souls from day to day,
Yet bids its votary revel in his gains,
Foul as the breath of drunkenness and lies.

The godless creed delights him much and long,
His mad design Jehovah to dethrone.
From Christian lands have gone the pagan shrines,
With all their rude and ruthless ministries.
Who worshipped there now stand or fall, each man
In his own lot.   Their way let none decry,
Though Satan near them held his seat of power,
Working in wantonness and cruelty,
Yet hiding his designs from souls deceived.
He was not banished when the temples fell,
But worketh yet in mysteries of sin.
The godless creed, his own by fatherhood,
Brings blatant bold denial for each truth
Endeared to hearts made loyal to their God.
Man it no more esteems than beasts that die,
But bids him find on earth his good supreme,
Nor dream of aught to recompense the just.
It gives no ray of hope to cheer the faint,
No sweet assurance of the Father's love,
No foretaste of enduring fellowship.

This godless creed is man's new cure for woe,
But, by denial, aggravates his pain,
While Satan laughs and mocks, his work well done
By such as bend true science to false ends.
Where the good thing which he hath not defiled,
The holy man whom he hath not assailed,
The worthy record not by him misread,
The charity which he hath not abused,
The truth ne'er sent by him to serve a lie ?

He works where laws unequal and unjust

Defy correction, by bold men upheld,
And where men who should guide affairs of state
Contend for place, forget the will of God,
And waste on needless things their time and ours.
   Alas, he, glozing, creeps within the Church,
That holy place where truth with charity
Must ever dwell, if Christ is to be pleased.
Where Satan works, see vanities displayed,
See veils conceal the truth that makes men free,
And charity sit down to sigh and mourn.
He works in all that feeds man's selfishness.
Who preach the cross and preach meanwhile themselves,
Their lore, their wealth of gifts, they hide the cross,
That glorious cross which crucifies the flesh,
And guides the soul through lowliness to God.
It pleases Satan to behold their ways,
Since service asked as pure is brought corrupt.
'Tis his fell work when greed of place and power
Makes better motives, poisoned by it, die,
And honour is reward for service done.
What love for God and man should send, in gifts
Spontaneous, to the sacred treasury,
Is drawn by promise of the printer's art,
Which publishes afar, that all may see,
The honoured name of him who gives to God.
   Thus Satan stains our sacred things, and men
Forget that gifts are as the heart that gives,
Worth measured by the weight of sacrifice,
Fame and its bellowing tongue as naught esteemed.
When will the morning dawn to see our aims

Let thus no more ?   Then shall reality
Be crowned as queen of all the ministries
Of saints, who will no longer weep to see
Corrosion creeping through the house of God,
To gnaw their holy things and make profane.

   If Satan finds prepared by man the soil
He loves, he sows, retires, and waits, his eye
No slumber knowing whilst the vile thing grows.
'Tis thus, though men heed not or deeply doubt.
What matters doubt to him who casts the seed ?
As cancerous blood all skill defies, and checked
Needs checking more, and thrives first here then there,
So Satan's seed, self-spread, is found unsought,
And subtly works, its strong root striking deep,
Till all the man is overrun, transformed,
And stands the body of a curse unknown.
First, sown in mind, the seed grows up a thought,
Condemned with might by conscience, guard divine
Of all the good of man.   Next, in the heart
The curse uplifts its form, and there, alas,
Is nourished with things precious which should make
An offering pure for heaven, and conscience now
Condemns more feebly.   Then at last the power
Executive in man, the will supreme,
The seed receives and welcomes ; and the man
Entire is soon quite overspread with rank
And noxious growths ; and conscience scarce can speak
Or breathe, its rights denied, its service scorned
Error and malice and defiance bold
Are fruit which nature, thus corrupted, bears.

So Satan works where pride of soul rejects
The truth of God, and slander moves the tongue
Of hatred, and true honour is denied
Both God and man, and selfishness sways all.
Who hath not seen such produce of his seed ?
Can nature be renewed in purity
And buoyant health, the devil's works destroyed,
That man may live the joyous liege of heaven ?

 Give ear and learn, ye patrons of the art
Of polishing man's nature unrenewed ;
How can an outward change make new the heart ?
Ye who delight to adore Humanity,
Behold your god, such as the gods of Greece,
In lies and hatred, fraud and blasphemy
O'erwhelmed ; and call to mind that he who prays
Grows like his god in character and life.
When will ye see how wayward is your creed,
How vain your fatuous hope of truer life ?

 And ye who trust to heal the maladies
Of man by what springs in him, pause. Know ye,
('Tis well to know,) the means ye so much prize,
Applied by minds sincere, have failed before.
The boldest flight of thought, the keenest search
In depths of philosophic gloom, the range
Gigantic of the intellect of man,
These hath the world already seen displayed,
Nor gained what ye would give by use renewed
Of that which stains the page of history
To man's disgrace. This truth to know, I ween,
Must now pertain to your true sciences.

Acknowledge this, and banish all your shame ;
Then see the folly of the course ye take,
And learn to speak in service of the truth
    Ye bold, who thought Humanitarian
And science, and the sweet persuasiveness
Of letters all despise, by your own art
Of cynic sneer and critic doubt demure,
Put faith aside, to leave an empty board
For hungry souls.   What profit have ye gained ?
Ye know man must obey, but choose for him
A lord unfit, unworthy quite to rule.
To Satan's work your doubt can bring no end ;
In such a soil it flourishes and spreads,
As weeds unchecked.   Can ye his power destroy ?
When doubt removes the poison of a lie,
Or bold denial ends a social curse,
Or yonder sun is darkened by the sleep
That shuts an infant's eye, then ye, by doubt,
May vanquish man's great foe, who works and reigns
Because his dupes refuse to see the cheat.
    All else can see the ruin he has wrought.
How may his mischief-working be withstood,
And how his ruinous designs o'erthrown ?
Ye lovers of mankind, attend, and leap
For joy, since man may be delivered.   How ?
    The answer hear, Jehovah's answer meet,
How fitly on this morn.   To earth has come
He who can vanquish hell and Satan's work
Destroy for evermore.   The friend of all,
He comes again to every faithful soul

And calls to share His glorious victory.
His birth surpasses all the wonderful.
No prodigy is here, but God is man,
The Infinite a babe !   Behold, he sleeps
In yonder stall.   Behold that gift of love
Which emptied heaven.   The Son of God is here
The Son of man.   Heaven's angels sing ; and we,
Listening, have heard again their notes prolonged
And all the nations yet the song shall learn.

  Pure from His birth, He knows no sin, no stain,
But lives in duty and in love for all,
In heaven while yet on earth.   He knows what none
Hath taught Him, and He hears and sees what man
Can not conceive.   In Him all righteousness
Is once for all fulfilled.   As prophet, priest,
And king divine, He bears anointing meet,
The Spirit given in blessing measureless,
Nay, infinite.
                God and His foes contend,
And, lo, the sword of truth prevails, and wins
Full victory for all.   Behold the Christ.
He comes to bless, to tell the thought of God,
To finish His great work, and open heaven.
He speaks, and grace entrances all that hear.
He meets the dumb, and, lo, the tongue is loosed.
The blind gropes to Him, lifts his eye, and sees.
Weakness, affrighted at His touch, withdraws,
And palsy, leprosy, and madness hear
His voice, and are no more.   The dead, when called
By Him, obeys and breathes again, and joy

Dries up the tears of grief. The hungry wait,
And in the wilderness a table, spread
By Him, gives plenty to a crowd. Though one
Small hand may bear what His glad helpers bring,
The arms of strength must carry what is left,
When thousands have their hunger satisfied.
To all the good His voice is harmony,
But grating discord in the heart untrue.
His life rebukes the vanities of man ;
And all, beholding, wonder who He is,
But many long to stay His arm of power,
While some curse oft the message of His lips,
And vow to shed His blood. The foe of man
Comes to Him, but naught finds in His strong soul
Responsive, and the craft and subtlety
Victorious oft are overcome for all.
The record finished and the witness made
Complete, He dies, the ransom of our race,
And opens wide the glorious gate of heaven.
Upon the Dead the grave is closed and sealed ;
But death is conquered, and the Conqueror lives.
Satan, thy throne usurped is trembling now,
And needs must fall, in witness of the truth,
Since Heaven's approval marks the Conqueror's work
With seal which none can break, none e'er remove.
    This warfare shall instruct the universe.
Go forth, ye men of God, and tell mankind,
This work complete, the way of life is free,
And grace to enter now and leave the paths
Of death, is offered unto all. Go forth.

The men obey, by love constrained to preach.
They tell to all what Jesus told to them,
And how He lived and died, and left the grave,
Went up to heaven to intercede for men,
And sent the Holy Ghost, the Paraclete,
Men to alarm, convince of sin, of right,
Of judgment, and the penitent to save,
In love divine which words can not declare.
Where'er they go they preach, and when they speak,
The Lord is nigh in wonders of His grace,
And Satan's works are openly destroyed.
Old things have passed away ; all things are new.
For falsehood truth, for fraud the love of right,
For vice all virtue, rise, to speak the power
Of grace divine ; and on the earth is seen
The life of heaven.   Justice adorns the house
That bears her name, and laws are ministries
Of love and peace.   Learning, a faithful guide
To truth, now waits to know the will of God.
Men speak the truth in love, and fear no ill ;
Authority is honoured and obeyed ;
For high and low pursue the paths of peace,
And stable are the sanctities of life.
In trade men handle what is lent by God,
In art true beauty is the child of prayer,
In church the voice well heard is Christ's own voice,
And in the state the welfare of mankind
Is guiding-star, nor ceases to be seen.
Love, peace, and joy (true inward heaven) abound
Where Jesus reigns.   O might He reign in all !

Our King still wars, and calls us to His side,
Since His great foe and ours is yet obeyed.
Can ye, O men redeemed, abet designs
Of woe by Satan laid ? Think not to say
Ye stand aloof, since each has part in this
Great contest, as is meet. A bitter curse
Once fell on men of Meroz, who had seen
The path of duty, and refrained their feet.
Beware lest such a curse fall on your head.
Be mindful of your part in this emprise.
Will ye prolong the tyranny which truth
Condemns, and have for master the usurping foe ?
The light of this glad day streams round the home
And through the mind, on earth the light of heaven.
Ye know the gift unspeakable. Behold
Its benefits outspread before your eyes
In gentlest charities of peace and love.
Trace ye the good beheld to yonder stall,
And thence to God's own heart ; and, Oh, beware,
Lest ye the grace of life refuse and die,
Heaven's portal standing open at your feet.
Come, take your joyous part in this great war,
And fight till victory is yours proclaimed.
Then shall ye see, and joy to see, the rule
Of Satan crushed and overthrown, and all
The saints in heaven with endless glory crowned,
God's purposes by all acknowledged wise.

MARGARET.

I do not like it ; he has preached too long.

LUCIA.

Sweet is the truth, and sweet that short discourse,
Which, to my soul, is like the scent of flowers.

REGNANS.

Grateful am I to hear a strong appeal
Based on the facts which none can now deny ;
And I am sure the preaching must do good.

ONE OF THE CROWD.

What is it all about ?   It wearies me.
I'll get away ; I wish I had not come.

ARETAS.

The Son of Mary is to conquer all,
And things that hurt the race must be removed.
On other ground I stand, but preach the same,
My true foundation still most firm and sure.
The preacher has not left me free from doubt,
But I, a leader, must regain and keep.
My confidence.   Humanity is great,
Supreme, divine !   And I, too, am a priest.

HERMES.

How inconsistent ! Their theology
Says what he preaches ; they do not the same.
If they believed such doctrines, could they look
Upon mankind distressed and do no more
Than now is seen ?   Where are the devil's works ?
Well, here, in most unchristian things by scores.

I'll write against the churches and the creed,
Decrying men whose words and ways conflict.
Why came I here to be anew displeased?
This teaching I can not at all endure;
I wish I might correct it in this fane,
Since misconceptions here grow rank like weeds.
But science will at length uproot them all.

LUCIDUS.

How sweet to me the form of that discourse.
In every part the light of letters shines
And glows.   But lost to me all faith in what
Was said.   Naught is theology that comes
In other garb than culture wears.   That bold
Appeal, which seemed to move the souls of some,
Left me without impression.   I have found
And know the sweet protection culture gives,
Nor can be moved by aught but gracious form.
That which is called the truth could move me once,
But I was young and had not found this light,
Nor knew protection as I know it now.

PHANE.

This service is a relic of that past
Which ever sinks into the vast abyss
Of dark oblivion, thence to rise no more.
What will replace the story of this day,
To serve the feeble mind, when Christmas dies?

HERMES.

The service ends, and I have heard enough,
More than enough, but yet must hear the hymn.

THE CHOIR.

Satan works, the heart deceiving,
    Folly rules, and wisdom weeps,
For he still the unperceiving
    In the toils of evil keeps.

Set them free, O Lord, from error,
    On their darkness pour the day ;
When they see their sins with terror,
    Turn their feet to wisdom's way.

Oh, how long we walk in sorrow,
    Walk by faith and not by sight,
Waiting for that promised morrow
    Thou shalt bless with perfect light.

Glad we join the host in singing
    Peace, good-will, and love to-day ;
Meet us, Lord, our homage bringing,
    Guide us on our homeward way.

X.—WHITECHAPEL.

[SUNDAY NIGHT.]

———

Where poverty with toil combines
  To quench the light of life,
Agnoscens, dreaming, sees the signs
  Of worse than mortal strife.
He goes where virtue never dwells,
  And watches, waits, and learns,
Till poignant grief his bosom swells,
  And shame his temple burns.

———

Richard. Margaret. Philippus. Carenda. Crowds.

Voices.

RICHARD.

What is the good of churches ?   There it stands
And takes up ground that might be turned to use.

MARGARET.

I wish they were destroyed, and in their place
Stood buildings fit to serve the poor.

PHILIPPUS.

When were
You in a church ?

MARGARET.

At Christmas I.

RICHARD.

And I,
I know not when.   I better like the play.
But, truth to tell, my great delight is here.

PHILIPPUS.

What is the house to which we go ?   Can you
Find room for me and my companion there ?

MARGARET.

Room ?   Ay, enough for you and more, and yet
The house is often full.

CARENDA.

What makes me shake ?
No one is here that knows me ; yet I feel
As if I touched my father's hand and heard
As when my mother calls me.   Yes, she says,
" Carenda, child, Oh, where are you, and who
Are your companions now ? "   And I have not
One word to say in answer.

ONE OF THE CROWD.

In they go,
Not all alike.` That shrinking girl is led,
And goes relunctantly.   She knows, I ween,
The better way and takes the worse, with pain
At heart.

ANOTHER.

What has the club done for him ? I
Well knew him in his better days.   I wish
His learned guides could see him here, as we,
And taste the produce of the seed they sow.

CARENDA.

You said you were at church at Christmas.   Where ?

MARGARET.

No matter where.

CARENDA.

Why did you tell us then ?
Which is the worse, that place or this, for such
As we ?

RICHARD.

How things have changed, and I have changed !
But stop such talk.   It suits not this our sphere.

SATAN.

I watch him well and oft have seen him here.
Deep is the hate and bitter are the tones
   With which he speaks of other scenes and days.

RICHARD.

I please myself ; my very flesh and bones
   Have left old courses for the freer ways
Of modern men. I read their books with care
   In other days, and found myself set free ;
And now I know not how at all to bear
   The simp'ring of the saints ; I want to see
All people follow nature, nor forswear
   Their birthright.

CARENDA.

      It is strange to me to hear
Such sentiment. What have we now to do
   With saints and men of prayer, for whom, I fear,
No proper berth is found with such a crew.
My early days come back. I ought to go,
   And never enter this dread place again.

RICHARD.

I have no patience with the useless flow
   From empty heads of hypocritic men,
Who preach a doctrine which they do not live,
   And live as now they live because they preach,
And cannot one convincing reason give

For what they say.   Be sure they will not reach
Men like myself, by all their talk and shew.
Let them learn but one half of what I know,
And they will laugh themselves to scorn, and soon
    Teach other doctrines and live other lives.

PHILIPPUS.

Too fiercely burns your anger.   Great the boon
    If all had knowledge ; but if one contrives
To leave the beaten track and take a course
    Such as you follow, what a cry there comes
Of wonder, pity, menace, and alarm !

MARGARET.

And yet what right has any one to force
Another ?   Surely 'tis no serious harm
    To please yourself.   That simple phrase but sums
The purpose of your nature, and no charm
    Is half so great or half so sweet.

CARENDA.

                              I see
That you have learned your lesson soon and well.
    I take it in but slowly, for to me
It looks just like a useless empty shell,
    That's called an egg, but holds no nutriment.
Sport as we will, man has a hungry soul
    That must be fed or die.   No nourishment
Is in these selfish doctrines.

PHILIPPUS.

> See this bowl ;
> Come, drink, and change your mind. You're too severe.

MARGARET.

You need no scruples when you meet us here.

RICHARD.

I please myself, and you must do the same.

PHILIPPUS.

Nor must we ever cross you in the game.

RICHARD.

I have been crossed, and shall be crossed again ;
> Whatever ye may do, myself I'll please.

CARENDA.

There is a way which leads to loss and pain.
> I know it, and am therefore ill at ease.

PHILIPPUS.

You say the truth, as we all know, but still
> We are not here to mope and whine. I think
There's something better for us. If you will,
> Just help yourself. Come, come, I wish you'd drink.

CARENDA.

I'll take a little just to please my friends.

MARGARET.

And I a little more for other ends.

RICHARD.

And I, to please myself as well as you.

PHILIPPUS.

And I, because I can no other do.

SATAN.

They like it, and have quite enough for all.
To that weak girl now comes a rapid fall.
   I let them take their course and need not strive,
   Since this the way to make my business thrive.
They urge themselves, and, stepping into thrall,
   What fools they are ; they know not where they go.
   But from the first it always has been so.

CARENDA.

The evening passes, and I must depart.

PHILIPPUS.

There is no need that you this moment start.
   I'll go with you and see you home ; but wait
A while and drink a little more ; it makes
   Us merry. I will read for you. I hate
All dulness.

CARENDA.

But this is the way of rakes.

RICHARD.

Who cares for that ? Pleasure was made for man.
  Come, drink, and let us chase our cares away.

MARGARET.

We're free, and on us here is no one's ban ;
  And I would here remain till break of day.

CARENDA.

I ought to go ; but let me hear this song ;
  It may be good as what they sing at church.

MARGARET.

But, be you sure, 'twill not seem half so long ;
  Else we for livelier rhymes should keenly search.

PHILIPPUS.

  We are strong and want no guide ;
  And the freedom here is wide
    For us all.
  Let us act then as we list,
  And on trifles not insist,
    Which enthral.

  Here no meadow tempts our feet,
  But our life is quite as sweet
    As is theirs
  Who are wending o'er the fields ;
  Nature all her treasure yields
    To her heirs.

We are heirs, and treasure find
In the beauty and the mind
    Of the fair.
Stay we here till morning light,
Living as it is our right,
    Free from care.

A Voice.

They mouth their song and work their will,
And of such things may take their fill
    As they prefer ;
With rules of prudence they dispense,
And think it joy to pamper sense.
    Alas, for her
Who bore a fainting witness here,
Which has been drowned in noxious beer
    And vinous thought.
Her moral limbs were growing lame ;
She fell outright when here she came,
    Her ruin wroug ht.

Carenda.

I'll sing for you a midnight song.
But why should I your watch prolong ?

Philippus.

Yes, sing, and tell us plainly how
Your Sunday simpering answers now.

CARENDA.

Come, all, and hear my voice,
    And let your laughter ring ;
Good reason why ye should rejoice
    My midnight metres bring.

Our youthful life is fleet,
    But lasting are our songs ;
Each other here we freely greet ;
    This right to us belongs.

Let those sing psalms and hymns
    Who know no joyous day ;
The sea of life he wisely skims
    That sails the easy way.

Why should we mope and moan,
    Oppressed with gloom and care,
And live like saints that pray and groan,
    No gladness anywhere ?

A VOICE.

Who waste their youthful strength,
    And drink, strength to renew,
Detect the cheat and sigh, at length,
    O'er pleasures faint and few.

The good of pampered sense
    Is weak and transient ;
The good that is the saint's defence
    Is strong and permanent.

I

Ye tempt your tempter here
    Upon a precipice.
How can ye, careless, stand so near ?
    Oh, hearken now to this :
Escape, or fall to death
    Where sorrow never dies ;
Better ye ne'er had drawn your breath,
    Ne'er gladdened mother's eyes.

SATAN.

Their song tells more than they intend or know.
But how they learn, and with what quick advance
Do they my work !   Philosophy and song
Dwell here together, and consort with shame.
My dupes these revellers are, and I am pleased.
What have they said wherewith I disagree ?
What have they done I can not well approve ?
Who now by saving them can thwart my ends ?
The sages see them not.   Poets of light
And sweetness and despair come not to note
The rip'ning of their crops, which now stand here
On ground prepared by those who chose the seed.
The harvest will be plenteous and the store
Immense of such as sow and all that reap.
How they will prize what they must then retain !
No more need I myself disturb.   Prate on,
Ye men of power, and send the heedless crowd
Astray, guiding the pliant will of sin.
My agencies, matured, will spread themselves,
And darkly work, while indignation rings

Through all the land ; for I have faithful slaves,
Whose rage, incarnate, strangest forms shall wear
Of cruelty, while horror clouds the face
Of young and old. Work on, and teach whom ye
Command.   If ye are mine, how many more
I claim, whose ways of vice shall shock the world,
When they to action turn what ye have said.

The godless creed stands sire of all the brood
Whose filth corrupts this city magnified,
The mother human nature, bred in sin,
And taught no help, no hope, no fear, no love.
Go, men, to do my work, and come to me
At length, and of my gloom of woe make heaven.
Long have I tried to make a heaven of hell,
And tried in vain.   Better can ye succeed,
When every check of grace divine has been
Withdrawn ?   No hope can then in you sustain
The effort of the will, but dark despair
The soul depress ; and to your cup of woe
Ingredients I will add which no relief
Shall give your bitterness.   It pleases me
To know your impotence.   Meanwhile I crave
No richer aid than yours, more fruitful none.

Work on apace, and let my kingdom spread,
That worlds may wonder at your recklessness.
But ye shall wonder most to see yourselves
In that clear light which ends the godless creed.
I know it can not live, for I believe
And quail.   But Satan's faith is godless still.
The truth of my own nature, once denied,

And cast away, I weened, for evermore,
Has now turned back upon my soul, and pains
As when a sword transfixes nerves of flesh ;
And I am father called of all the false,
By Him whose word for ever stands secure.
Can ye your truth deny and meet no woe ?
Can ye be mine and never curse yourselves ?
Your bold defiance waits its due reproof.
Meanwhile ye serve me well, your vengeful king.

XI.—A PLEASURE GARDEN.

[SUMMER EVENING.]

———

Agnoscens sings with those who sing,
    And laughs with them that laugh.
Oh, what delight his visions bring
    While all the nectar quaff,
That flows where youth in freedom walks,
And of pure nature's purpose talks !

———

Carolus. Stephanas. Regnans. Lucia. Optatus.
Blanda. Probus. Docendus.

OPTATUS.

A glorious day declines in tranquil eve,
    And ere the shades ascend we rest and talk.

CAROLUS.

A finer day than this, I do believe,
    Ne'er shone on me since I began life's walk.

BLANDA.

Come, read the songs ye penned
When ye would all contend

In making verse.
If ye rehearse
What has been set in form to-day,
The rest will find somewhat to say.

OPTATUS.

Sweet the breeze that blows perfumed
　　From yonder bank of roses ;
Sweet the bleating of the lamb
　　That near the bank reposes ;
Sweet the song of soaring lark,
　　Streaming in joy and sunshine ;
Sweet the sight of tiny moss
　　Or green, or grey, or rubine ;
Sweet the care with which the dam
　　Gives to her young protection ;
Sweet the lowing of the herd
　　That yields our rich confection ;
Sweet the face of earth and sky
　　Whene'er the bard has vision ;
Sweet the powers of mind to try,
　　Work choosing with precision ;
Sweet the joy of heart at ease ;
　　Yea, peace on earth with heaven
Sweeter is than scented breeze
　　Here wafted on you seven.

DOCENDUS.

The light that shines o'er earth and sky
　　Shines for the souls of men ;

It visits every open eye
   On mountain, sea, or fen.

It makes no sight, but finds in each
   What answers to its touch ;
Minutest crevice it can reach ;
   Little it is or much,

As need may be. The insect's wing
   It paints, and guides its eye ;
Stupendous systems poets sing
   It fills, both far and nigh.

The light of mind is fair to see,
   For culture brightens all
That sets the powers of manhood free
   From wrong and folly's thrall.

But fatuous is the light that shines
   Where learning is profane,
And culture but the heart inclines
   In folly to remain.

True wisdom is where beams the light
   That comes when sought in prayer ;
Who finds it glories in that sight
   Which doth for heaven prepare.

PROBUS.

From the depths of dark despair
   Comes to-day the voice of song :
Strange to us that culture there
   Can its being thus prolong.

We have heard the piteous cry,
  Loud, and passionate, and deep,
Wond'ring that philosophy
  Can her seat in darkness keep.

Dark for light the poet brings,
  Gloomy fear for joyous trust ;
Misery he sweetly sings,
  Beauty gives to thoughts unjust.

Perfect peace is in the soul
  Calmed by grace through fervent prayer ;
Pitiful the self-control
  Of the poet of despair.

REGNANS.

Just are their thoughts, and I have heard with joy
  What has been read. Think you the same with me ?

LUCIA.

How oft such themes the active minds employ
  Of my good brothers. They have come to see
How empty are the things that some admire.

REGNANS.

And in their souls there burns a strong desire
  To check men's error and teach better ways.
The work is needed, and I hope the fire
  Will burn more and yet more. In dark sad days
When blasphemy abounds, we sorely need
  Men of conviction, zeal, and power to cope
With what they find.

LUCIA.

True, it is so indeed,
And I believe good reason is to hope
My brothers will be such, and will defend
    The truth, and put gainsayers to the blush.

REGNANS.

I dare believe they will ; but to contend
    With men of science who in boldness rush
To scorn the creed and overthrow the truth,
    Is work which needs a giant's strength.   I find
Not all that try can do this work.

LUCIA.

                                In youth
    It must be so.   Yet when his gifts of mind
A man devotes, and works his best, we bless
    The deed and laud the aim.

REGNANS

                            Well, walk along
This path with me, not grieving if they guess
    What we intend.   'Tis known we now belong
Each to the other, and must talk apart
    Of our affairs.

LUCIA.

They will not grudge us this.

BLANDA.

Yes, they have gone to stroll.   I will not start
　To follow them.   But may they find pure bliss
In every pathway till they pass above.

CAROLUS.

Bliss will be found if they pursue the ways
Of truth, where flourish all the flowers of love.
Who walk by faith in God meet happy days.

STEPHANAS.

Some walk to woe below, and downward draw
　Their fellows.   How I wish they could but go
Alone.

CAROLUS.

　　Alas, they do not care one straw　　[know
　If suff'ring spreads.   They please themselves and
Their time is short.   It makes me grieve to see
　Such heedless work.   I mourn as I reflect
On all the ways that ignorant folly takes ;
　But learned folly is the worst of all.
It plants, with words of grace, its noxious tree
　Where it is known men will not long neglect
To gather what is borne.   'Tis this that makes
　The friends of truth despondent, great and small.
What will the end of all this folly be ?

BLANDA.

Heard ye the news that has, alas, come down
Since we met here to-day ?   Richard has gone.

CAROLUS.

Gone !   Where ?

BLANDA.

    To death. He died, we hear, in town,
Died a most shameful death by his own hand.

STEPHANAS.

Keen intellect through his strong features shone
    And lustrous eye.   But soon I marked a frown,
Which looked defiance, when he joined that band
And took its ways.   Alas, alas !   But how
Came he to die ?

BLANDA.

    He could not meekly bow
When trial came, and seek the help of God.
    He boasted he was strong, and said his will .
Was firm, and he would have his way, though now
    Passion was his stern master, and he still
Went down and down and down ; so, at the nod
    That ends the day of grace, he hopeless fell,
    Self-thrown, yea, slain by his own hand.   Oh, tell
It everywhere, and warn the young, not yet
    Enslaved to drink and passion and that vain
Philosophy which mocks the truth.

STEPHANAS.

        We get
In this a glimpse of what will come to stain

Our country's fame, when that subversive force
   Which now is seen at work has reached its end.
Richard has run a bold and rapid course.
   How weak is man when he dares to contend
Against the laws of God !

BLANDA.

                  Alas, one drew
  Him on whom he had ruined first.   She tried
To drag down others and had some success.

STEPHANAS.

That he had wandered far full well we knew,
  But trusted still he a clear path descried
Whereby he might return, the hand to bless
  (Of love and mercy) that should bring him home.
It is too late.   It yet remains to learn
  Such lesson as we may, lest we, too, roam
And find against us holy vengeance burn.

OPTATUS.

He lived to please himself, though well he knew
His days, the law of health transgressed, but few
Could be.   He followed well his guides, and paid
The penalty of scorn.   Thus has he made
His life a sacrifice to base desires
Which scorched him day and night like with'ring fires.
The juice of life is lost if faith depart,
And false philosophy dry up the heart.
O that his teachers knew what he had learned ;

PROBUS.

And that he long ago their books had burned ;

BLANDA.

And that men would but seek their fellows' weal ;

STEPHANAS.

And not their birthright by fair falsehood steal.

CAROLUS.

Then would their onward course be straight and pure,
    And life, a blessing made, be full of good,
Which must from age to age on earth endure,
    Like some great rock that has through tempests stood.

OPTATUS.

Would men of years but tell us how to think
    Of this bold age which boasts of what it knows.
        Is faith to die before the human race
Has run its course ?   I am amazed and shrink
    At what I fear.   Rank social mischief grows,
        And great the need that stern rebuke should face
Impurity and lies, with their long train
    Of offspring.   Would they were o'erturned, as when
        A mighty wind lays low a tottering wall.
The fate of Richard fills our hearts with pain,
    Diminishing our feeble hope for men,
        And makes us wonder who will trust recall.
The men whose thought is ripe may aid us much,
If they on earth of heaven have conscious touch.

Blanda.

Men may lose faith, but women yet will trust.

Optatus.

But will they trust in God ?   The faith we need
Is that.   O'er modern thought has grown a rust
Which eats into the substance of the creed.

Blanda.

I can not reason, and I will not try
    To work persuasion by the art of words ;
But I can feel ; and day and night I cry
    To God, as streams the ceaseless song of birds,
By nature taught.   Believe a woman's heart,
    Nor think she can not feel the thought of God.
Woman, if true, will choose the better part ;
    Woman, when false, must bear the heaviest rod ;
Woman will teach her lisping child to pray ;
    And woman, won to Christ, will gently guide
The infant's feet in paths of peace.   I say,
    O men, while woman lives faith must abide.
Striplings are vain and wander from their weal,
Because they heed not what true mothers feel.

Probus.

The point is proved ; I like the argument.

Optatus.

But there are men who are not thus content.

STEPHANAS.

What want they more than woman's feeling claims
In words that have this moment shewn her aims ?
She feels her need, and prays, and so believes
That evidence is in what she receives.
Sister such feeling is to true content ;
And let no man despise this argument.

CAROLUS.

That many find ; but help they sorely need
Who lack such woman's faith. It is agreed
That there are rocks round which sore wrecks are strewn
Because the course of safety was unknown.

DOCENDUS.

The soul is held by sweet restraint of grace,
   And faith then conquers all ; nor in the dark
Will sail the child of God. Give ample space
   To reason, but let faith direct the barque
O'er life's mysterious main. Then will your course
Be safe, though tempests spend on you their force.

STEPHANAS.

Reason and faith us to allegiance call.
   On clearest grounds God bids all men believe,
   And wealth of bliss the obedient now receive,
And will retain. Before them mountains fall
Or are removed, as they pursue their way.
   Who forfeits reason and then boasts to find
   That faith is dead, is cheated by his mind,
And thinks it night when round him shines the day.

He that believes the peace of God hath found ;
  He that believes hath calm for mental strife ;
  He that believes discerns the end of life ;
He that believes hath proved his reason sound.
Believe, because God bids thee, and because
Thy reason urges, " Follow nature's laws."

OPTATUS.

The day has gone, and bird and beast and flower
    Are all in deep repose ;
And we must part.   Hereafter many an hour,
    As lives the fragrance of a rose,
The themes we have discussed, both sweet and sour,
    Whereof some came and some we chose,
Must still be pondered as we have the power.

SATAN.

I hate such warning songs ;
    I hate the guard of prayer ;
To my soul it belongs,
    And is my constant care,
To make it hard to hope,
    And harder to believe,
The power with sin to cope
    Man may on earth receive.
But when a woman feels
    And calls her feeling faith,
Naught but the sin that steels
    Can gainsay what she saith.

I overcome the fools
 Who know no better way
Than to be abject tools
 Of thoughts that lead astray.
But here are those who look
 To God for constant aid,
And learn from His own book
 The path for virtue made.
In spite of me they stand
 Pure as in rosy youth.
I hate what stays my hand,
 I hate God's saving truth.

XII.—THE COTTAGE ON THE HEATH.

———

Beauty blooming at his side
In the glories of a bride,
Anguish speaking through a face
Once suffused with maiden grace,
Wrongs that crush a wasted life
Where should be the happy wife,
In his dream, Agnoscens these
Clearly and in sorrow sees.

———

Regnans. Lucia. Docendus. Blanda. Optatus. Emilia.

BLANDA.

The bride was beautiful and all went well.

OPTATUS.

The service was perfection.   I will tell
   Our friends in town, by telegraph, to save
Them doubt.

BLANDA.

       Lucia, I say, was truly brave,
And Regnans took his part in worthy style.
   No wedding ever pleased me half so much.

DOCENDUS.

I wish another soon might please her more.

LUCIA.

The story of the day I will compile
 And send to town. Oh, it will sweetly touch
The hearts of all our friends.

DOCENDUS.

      There is a store
Of good for some one in that soul. It glows,
And dazzles me, as nothing e'er before.
 Who, that loves not, such rapture ever knows ?

OPTATUS.

How I was tried when I must give away
 A sister always good and dear to me.

BLANDA.

She will be truly happy, you shall see ;
And Regnans has been fortunate to-day.

EMILIA.

As we passed through the crowd I saw a form
 That made me think of school, and early days,
And those who knew me then. But, Oh, the storm
 Has bruised her, and the marks of evil ways
Were on her face. Alas, poor Margaret !

BLANDA.

I saw her too, and sighed.   May she not yet
   Be saved ?   Turning my face away, I felt
A tear was mingling with our joy.

OPTATUS.

                           'Tis but
A little while since all the ways seemed shut,
   For her, of strong temptation.   Quickly melt
The most approved protections when the heart
   Is bad.   A curse must rest on Richard's head.

EMILIA.

Oh, wickedness !   She took a willing part
   In that man's life, who now is with the dead.
I blame her much, but pity more.   The lot
Is sad of her who sins with cultured sot.

OPTATUS.

His powers were wasted.   How he read and drank,
  Then cursed and raved, till all he had was spent !
His theories of man and life were rank
   With bestial passion ; and, we know, he went
With headlong speed to death, and, on the way,
   Dealt out destruction where he could ; and she,
Whose lot we know and weep, his victim lay
   An off'ring which it pains the soul to see.

BLANDA.

Is there no hope that she may still be saved ?

Much would I do her sunken life to raise. .
We know she has most wickedly behaved,
   And should henceforth go mourning all her days ;
But she's our sister, and true Christian care
Might save her yet from merited despair.

DOCENDUS.

Most gracious soul !　How happy he that gains
   Companionship with thee.　My glowing heart
Has felt a mystic touch that subtly pains
   While it gives pleasure.　O that I could dart
My honest thought, and make her know my mind,
And then our lives in common welfare bind.
No prince amidst the splendours of a throne
Would be so happy, were that soul my own.

EMILIA.

The case, I fear, is hopeless.　Vice and sneers
   Make triple conquest o'er mind, heart, and will.
How can she love whose heart is quite depraved ?
   How can she think in whom vice domineers ?
How can she choose aright whose passion still
Absorbs her life ?　How can such souls be saved ?
Do for her what ye may.　Gravely I doubt
If vict'ry e'er can follow such a rout.

DOCENDUS.

The other's speech was sweet, but this is sour
   To me, though it may tell the truth.

EMILIA.

I fear

The age wherein we live must feel the power
   Of vice, since those new doctrines which appear
To some so hopeful are not checked and blown
   Away.   Richard was great in his own eyes,
And Margaret was flattered and o'erthrown
   By plausibilities of pride, and lies
Corrupting.   He has died by his own hand,
   But she is dedicate to basest work,
And lives by infamy, and now may stand
   A warning to her sex.   While spy and lurk
Betrayers everywhere, small is the hope
   That one so weak, made weaker by her ways
And weaker still, will ever rise to cope
   With her enthralment.   Now the price he pays
Of culture steeped in sin ; and she has passed
   Beneath the yoke of an economy
Which o'er her such a gloom of woe hath cast
   As words can not describe.   From infamy,
Oh, save her, if ye can.   Ye may succeed ;
But great the wonder when such slave is freed.

DOCENDUS.

She reasons like a man, and may be right.

BLANDA.

The friends whose joy of love we bless to-day
   Have gone from us, and we have seen a sight
Which points a contrast painfully complete.

DOCENDUS.

Sweet are the words her lips of beauty say.

BLANDA.

'Tis true we can not save her by the might
Of man.   Such lives philosophy defeat
   And trample in the mire.   But we can go
To the Omnipotent whose love is great
   And reaches all ; and He by grace may shew
Her better ways, and lead into the state
   Of life renewed by power divine.   Despair
Becomes us not.   If we believe that when ·
   We cry to God He hears our prayer,
Why may not we, as Daniel while the den
   Of lions yawned, prevail, and Margaret
From all her snares deliver ?   How I long
   To tell her of God's love, and clearly set
Her good in view.   For this God make me strong !
Still lives the love that saved the Magdalene
From bondage great as aught that she hath seen.

DOCENDUS.

Through inspiration coming from above,
The savour of this character is love.
Hemmed in are sages where her love sees way,
And what to them is dark she finds as day.
Her faith is mighty and will surely win,
And thereby Margaret be saved from sin.
Were there a faith like this in every breast,

Mankind would bow with joy to God's behest.
O˙were this heart of faith and love made mine !
With growing brightness how my days would shine !

Emilia.

I say, Amen, and hope against the fears
    That rise within my heart. But God is good.
Great blessing rest on her who goes in tears
    To raise a sister fallen ! I have stood
To watch the work of sin as seen in street
    And dusky lane of our great city, till
My heart grew sick, and anguish made me beat
    My breast, and seek relief where I seek still,
In home; my home. There love and gentle care
    Have ever guarded me. What I have seen
Makes slight my hope for Margaret. I dare
    Not doubt the grace of God. I have not been
So long upheld and saved, without a deep
    Knowledge and sense of its stupendous worth.
And well I know the Lord will always keep
    The soul that trusts in Him.

Optatus.

                      Of heavenly birth
Are saving thoughts. Who runs to dry the tear
    Of lonely grief is messenger of love.

Blanda.

Who waits on God till grace is found to cheer
    The downcast, is as angel from above.

But she who touches Margaret, to raise
  Her being to the plane of purity,
Receives, where honour goes with truth, the praise
  Of likeness to the Lord himself ; for He
Such work achieves by those who trust.   Do this,
And you shall share His secret of true bliss.

DOCENDUS.

In love of truth her womanhood now shines,
And no false modesty her thought confines.
She doubts and reasons like a man of sense,
Seeing a task before her quite immense.
Now I must tell my thoughts and speak aloud,
Nor longer be as one enwrapped in cloud,
Obscure, mysterious, dark.   What is the use ?
At last my thoughts must flow, my lips be loose.

EMILIA.

Much more am I inclined to seek her good ;

DOCENDUS.

And help to save her I most gladly would.

EMILIA.

I pitied her as in the street she stood,
  And looked on us in our most diverse state.

OPTATUS.

How many, failing, on their fortune wait,
And long and have not, day by day, through life ;

Nor thrift, nor care, nor wisdom blesses them.
　Such yield themselves to what is deemed their fate,
And judge that naught is worth the ceaseless strife
They in their neighbours see, who currents stem
　Of care and hardship.

BLANDA.

　　　　　　Let me know how I
May raise a fallen life and Margaret
　To her first ways restore.

EMILIA.

　　　　　　On God rely,
And do your best.　'Tis true that she has yet
　Some hope of years; but, Oh, that record black
Which she has written and can not erase!
　The blood of souls is on her awful track.
I marvelled not that woe looked through her face;
　I should have marvelled had she seemed serene.

BLANDA.

Torment and strife have long her portion been.

OPTATUS.

Not long but swift has been the course of sin.

DOCENDUS.

Will you at once your work of love begin?

BLANDA.

I will begin if I can find her home.

EMILIA.

Through many a scene of sin expect to roam.

BLANDA.

Shall gladly bear it all to gain my end.

DOCENDUS.

Go, work your best, and you may Heaven forefend.
In freeing that poor sister from her thrall
You witness for the Lord, who loves us all.
A curse came on her through philosophy
When she was snared by one whose sophistry
The men who taught him can not vindicate.
He read their books, and learned their views to state,
And shewed those views in practice day by day,
And boasted much of freedom.   Who can say
Where ends the curse of that one wasted life,
Which reached at length the self-inflicted knife ?
Why should it not, if there were naught beyond
The limits of our sense ?   The living bond
Of flesh is snapped, and then, say they, the end !
But is that end the blank which they describe
Who this new sweet philosophy imbibe,
And boast of freedom while they aimless roam,
Like children proud to have escaped from home ?

OPTATUS.

If Richard's guides should you this day attend,
How would you reason now as friend with friend ?

DOCENDUS.

Oh, I am pained, and hot my words would be,
In this bold strain :

     O men, do ye not see
Your doctrine's fruit ? Gives it you joy or pain
That one who followed you himself hath slain ?
Blame ye the wretch that hastens from his woe ?
Was it not wise that he with haste should go,
Since man going is gone, and is no more,
In any sense, in any world ? Behold,
Here trace your doctrine out ; else seeming bold
Ye are but cowards. Sum your teaching up.
How reason ye of one who drinks the cup
Of pleasure, taught by you, as Richard drank ?
Shall we, or shall we not, his teachers thank ?
Oh, see the truth ye should have seen long since,
And let that truth your anxious minds convince.
Can that be good which fostered Richard's vice ?
Can it be worth what he has paid, the price
Of his own ways ? Can ye, as men, defend
The doctrine held by him to that sad end ?

  Why ran ye not to save him from his fate ?
Why run ye not to-day to save his mate ?
See ye the zeal displayed by Christian minds ?
It seeks and seeks, until at last it finds,
The object of concern, not sparing pains,
Though obloquy or hate be all it gains,
Until at last it turns from sin and crime
The soul redeemed, to live beyond all time
In God's own heaven. With that great work compare

What ye have done.   Are ye ashamed, or dare
Ye boast as friends of man ?   What ye can do
We see in Richard, who, proud of his crew,
Boasted of liberty, in fetters bound,
And thought he soared when sinking to the ground.
On culture's height with you we may not stand,
Nor do we wish to join your boastful band ;
But we have heard a voice ye never heard,
Have felt constraints which ne'er your souls have stirred,
Beheld a light which ye have never seen,
Walked upon paths where ye have never been,
And known a strength which ye have never sought.
The good ye value most we count as naught.
Your doctrines havoc work and breed despair,
Denying comfort to the child of care.
Why walk ye in a chosen path of gloom
When near you streams pure light, and ample room
Is offered you with those whose paradise,
As free from doubts tormenting as from vice,
Is shining with the glory of the word
Of Him whose voice the saints by faith have heard ?
How weak is man unstrengthened with His might,
Groping, confused, shut out from truth's pure light !
Why scorn ye then the day and choose the night ?

BLANDA.

A happy day !
Our friends the God of grace will lead,
And on their chosen pathway speed.
For them we pray.

And may we give
Long as we live
Attention to the need
Of those whom vice or greed
Has led astray.

XIII.—BURLINGTON HOUSE.

As one who runs
On crowded road,
And deftly shuns,
In changing mode,
The human forms that swarm around,
So is Agnoscens, dreaming, found.
While sages block the way with facts
And plead the merit of their acts,
He hears them called in true belief
Their souls to save
From doubt's dim care.
He dreams they never seek relief.
Oh, how he mourns with honest grief !

Hermes. Dardan. Phane. Aretas. Lucidus. Victor.
Quaerens. Doctus.

VICTOR.

We must have facts ; else we shall quite misjudge.

HERMES.

And I have gathered facts and trust in them,
But nothing else.

LUCIDUS.

          And facts must be arranged
In literary form to meet the taste
Of culture.

ARETAS.

       What is form?   Let us have truth,
And it may take that form which suits it best.
Man is immortal, and his richest thought
Lives with him, treasured in the race, from age
To age.   Humanity is reverend.

DOCTUS.

But is it reverent?

ARETAS.

       Yes, it reveres
Itself, as is most meet ; and all the spots
Called sin will disappear, as specks of dust
Pass from a garment plunged in purging stream.

PHANE.

Consistent doctrine ! Bring us now the facts.
Think ye they will support the doctrine taught ?

DARDAN.

Let me begin.   The Holy Church is one.
The Pope must settle facts and doctrines too.
Without his sign philosophy is vain ;
And science can not prosper when he frowns ;

And facts mislead if he but disapproves.
Be Catholic, or ye can not be saved.
Young science changes every hour, and men
By contradiction live.   I like the way
Which settles, once for all, theology
And life.

SATAN.

His doctrine, well applied, will freeze
Up all the energy of man, and much
Help me in my design.   I hope he will
Persuade them he is right.   Then I shall toil
The less, and rest the more, and have fresh ground
For my sad joys.

PHANE.

Your theory is vain.
The story of the Church condemns outright
All notions of the kind.   Now ye may bring
The facts.   Shew how the doctrine works.   Disclose
The solid rock on which he safely stands
Who plants his feet.

DARDAN.

The facts lie as I said.

QUAERENS.

He gropes and nothing finds, but fancies much,
Believes, affirms, and says, " Behold, the Church
Has taught me, and the Holy Church is true,

And cannot err." We want to know the facts.
A fatuous guide would lead us all astray.
We are not children, but now claim the rights
Of men.

SATAN.

I hate the science ne'er content.

DARDAN.

I should despise this life were there no Church
Infallible.

PHANE.

No Church infallible
There is ; but we have life, and like its good,
And live as other men at ease.   The ills
Which we so much deplore are bearable.
This frankly we confess; and life is worth
The living.   Let us know.   We wait for facts.

DOCTUS.

And I am here to state facts for the aid
Of all.   Richard, ye know, is dead.   He died
In town by his own hand.

SATAN.

                        What have they now
To do with Richard ?   He is safe with me.
I wish they might forget him evermore.

DOCTUS.

He read your books and made his boast of your
Philosophy, setting in word and deed
Your views of life and duty, teaching some
To do the same, and boasted he was free.
What was his freedom ?   Down he went and down,
From deep to deep of vice and infamy,
Degraded and degrading.

ARETAS.

         But he should
Have lived a better life.

DOCTUS.

         Well, why, if he
But chose what pleased him and naught is beyond
The blank of death ?   Why should a man distress
Himself for naught ?

SATAN.

         My soul in me is vexed.
Why questions he of things they can not know ?
I hate such speech.   Men must be kept from ways
Bold and straightforward.

ARETAS.

         Let us now be clear.
Humanity has claims which he despised.
'Tis rev'rend and divine, and must advance.

Doctus.

Richard has told who taught him what he did ;
And who can now disprove the witness borne ?

Aretas.

Instead of cursing by his vicious ways,
He should have lived to bless his fellow men.
Before his eyes the path of duty lay,
And well he knew he should have been a guide.

Doctus.

Why should he ?   Where is such authority
As is supposed ?   Who had the right to change
Or check the course of passion in his life ?
The freedom he had learned of you he loved,
And prized, and used.   Who had the right to lay
Restraint upon him, who ? . Adduce your facts,
And let us know the truth, nor judge amiss.

Aretas.

In Richard all benevolence was dead.

Doctus.

Died his benevolence, or was it slain ?
He said he followed you and such as ye.
Was his benevolence then slain by you ?
Can ye disprove the charge implied ?

ARETAS.

Think not
To baffle me.   Humanity is great !
Let Richard pass, and let his place be filled
More worthily.   The race is limitless.
This mighty tree must flourish ; it can spare
The useless branch, whether it fall as he
Or be removed as when a criminal
Endures the penalty of death.   He lived
In vice, and died as he had lived.

DOCTUS.

What right
To call it vice to follow nature as
He followed it ?   Who makes it wrong to please
The senses as he pleased ?   If in some state
Men live like brutes and pamper sense, can ye
Inflict rebuke and bid them change their lives ?
Whose is the ground whereon ye stand to speak
Your law ?   Men who serve sense must promptly call
You trespassers, and bring you down, and bid
You name your master and his right, or stand
In muteness by, nor sway their will.   And why
Should ye disturb their pleasure ?   Ye profess
To serve Humanity ; they do the same.
Your god's your neighbour ; theirs is but themselves.
What difference makes the paper shrine ye build
Of books which men admire ?   In grief or joy,
In loss or gain, they and yourselves agree
For man to live.   This doctrine may displease.

Disprove it if ye can ; if not, be mute.
We ask the honest sense of patent signs ;
And Richard's life and death are staring facts.
What is the theory that takes them in,
That reconciles their horror with your boast,
And makes you calm when they before you lie ?

PHANE.

They well deserve this orthodox rebuke,
And must needs meet such rational demands.

ARETAS.

I much dislike this new dogmatic way.

DARDAN.

And I prefer the true Infallible,
But need not say again what I have said.

HERMES.

I have no Church, no faith, and yet my joy
Is, that I teach and help my fellow men.
I can not find the reason, but I feel
Constraint, and am impelled.   The vast unknown
Is wonderful to me, and much of what
I see is wondrous too ; but vice I hate
With all the strength of an embittered mind.
My good is thought, which mystic power distils
In the obscure impalpability
Of brain and nerves !   This deep prolonged research
Leaves much how dark !   But I have hope to chase
The mists and shew the day.

PHANE.

       The day will shew
Itself ; if not, your dense inscrutable
Impalpability of words bombast,
In which ye tell us what is life, yet fail
To make us know, will never clear the sky.
Light is a glory which itself reveals.
But I impatient am of thought obscure.
Tell us the truth, though it may bring you shame,
And let us have that light which needs no lamp.
Richard is dead ; who taught him how to die ?

HERMES.

My nature pities Richard and all such
As he, who wrong themselves and wrong the race.
They put on all our theories a stain
Which we resent. Had Richard followed me,
He had done well. My doctrines want no creed
To buttress them ; they rest secure on facts,
My own through toil of years.

PHANE.

        A bubble blown
Into the air mounts loftily, and, lo,
It glistens in the light, and children clap
Their hands in sportive glee. Men toil, and sweat,
And wonder at their works.

HERMES.

       This toil of mine
Is for the good of man. Some heed it not ;

But I can wait for recognition due.
My time will come.   The worthless willow shoots
To its perfection, but the precious oak
Grows slowly, and adorns its native scene
Five hundred years.

PHANE.

       The bubble rises fair and bursts ;
And then the children blow another.   How
They laugh and shout to see it soar on high
More beauteous than the first.   While they exult,
Behold, it is no more.

HERMES.

       It pains me much
To be misunderstood.   Colossal toil,
Like mine, is worthy, and shall have its meed
Of praise.   Meanwhile I wait in confidence,
And seek the good of man.

PHANE.

       Oh, bring us facts.
You are reluctant ; then give heed to me.
Richard is dead, who had no faith, no hope.
He, too, lived for the good of man,—himself.
What could the creed have done to make him worse ?
Would faith have dimmed his vision of the good,
Or hope have brought such gloom as his sad end ?
What has he gained through all your boundless toil ?
Who can be proud of what he learned and did ?

He named his teachers and was proud to name.
They sowed in him the seed whose fruit we see.
I bring you facts.

SATAN.

These critics vex my soul.
How can my work succeed, except they fail ?
Let me confound them by the sins they love,
That they, deceived, may trust themselves alone.

HERMES.

Had Richard followed me, he had not gone
So far astray in waste of life. Alas,
Perverseness mastered him and laid him low,
When true philosophy had held him up ;
And in my life he might have seen the way.

PHANE.

Men's lives are seen by few ; but books reach all,
First those who read, then those whom they affect.
Who feels not thus the savour of a book ?
Your influence works where men know not your face.
All vice ye hate, but that is no excuse
For doctrines which men easily pervert,
And which, 'tis said, are enemies to prayer,
And lead no soul to trust the love of God.

LUCIDUS.

But we must still our liberty maintain ;

ARETAS.

Nor let fantastic teachers cause us fear,
Since we have found the true Infallible,
And contradictions can be reconciled,
For there is one to guide through all disputes.

PHANE.

How well ye love the contradiction sweet !
How could ye live if it were once removed ?
How can ye die while it may be prolonged ?
What, if ye die by your own sweetness killed ?
Then will the truth have come for you in vain.

LUCIDUS.

We clearly tend, poor things, some other way
When called to righteousness. There is a power
That helps us, but there is another power
Which hinders good.

DOCTUS.

　　　　　But what is righteousness ?
Who gave its nature and its limits fixed ?
And who will punish us if we neglect ?
Is it a thing or but a word, which each
May for himself explain ? Authority
Must somewhere dwell. Does God our Father hear
The prayer of faith and save the soul of man ?
Your creed of words not things, of sounds not truths,
Creates no faith. What can it do for me ?

LUCIDUS.

It overthrows some useless fables, taught
In every age by poets and the Church.

PHANE.

But did those fables touch our Richard's life ?
He had been taught at home the love of truth,
And spake to God in prayer as to a friend.
Not long ; but truth and prayer led him not down
To vice, and shame, and suicide. He lost
The truth when he gave up the form of words
Prescribed, pretending by the wording new
To guide to thought more true, more clear. What gain ?
The autumn leaf takes beauty from decay,
The child is blessed through discipline of love,
And faithful castigation makes the book ;
But nature left unpruned is wild and waste ;
And whoso builds an altar of his words
And on it offers truth, is judged unwise.
Who follows nature in her waywardness
But mars what he should make, virtue's firm fence,
And wonders as he sees his foolishness.

LUCIDUS.

For me the doctrine is too Churchmanlike.
We must our liberty of speech maintain ;

HERMES.

And liberty to print what we have thought ;

DARDAN.

And through the Church t' interpret what we read ;

DOCTUS.

And to correct the errors of the vain ;

PHANE.

And to rebuke the vanity of men
Who deem that true which they affirm.

DOCTUS.

Who boast
They have no master, and no Church, no creed,
No fear, no hope, must float like guideless ship
On dark and stormy sea.   They know nor whence
They came nor where they go.

PHANE.

Ah, yesterday
They were not, and to-morrow will have gone ;
But the vast sea of facts will heave the same.
Alas, they are philosophers.   They say
And do not ; yea, they contradict, and do
What they deny.   They boast and tremble now.
Their boasting is of freedom, deeply prized ; [heaven
The trembling comes with thoughts of death and
We measure greatness by the fear it rules ;
Great are they but in restless unconcern.

SATAN.

He may have meant those words to point to me.

PHANE.

The day has dawned when they must be rebuked
With fearlessness, and called to see themselves
As they are seen where shines the light of truth.

DOCTUS.

But will they ever see so much ?   The light
Of truth shines where it is made welcome.   He
Who yearns to do the will of God shall know
That will, but whoso lives to please himself,
And boasts of liberty, owning no God,
Errs far, and will to-morrow wander more.
Alas, do they not hate that truth which shines
For all ?   How can they know the mind of God ?

SATAN.

How hot this zeal !   He burns his friends with words.
Why is he not content to live at peace
With men whose views gainsay his own ?   He might
Let them untroubled live and peaceful die.

DOCTUS.

Their state is seen, displayed in what they do.
Have they at heart the welfare of their kind ?
Where then the sign of true fraternal care ?
The millions die betrayed, o'erwhelmed in sin.
What millions will repeat themselves !   The race,
While individuals pass away, still lives.
What gains it from philanthropists who sit,
Their minds at ease, and gaze around ?   They say,

" Naught can we do to stem this ceaseless tide ;
It comes and goes we know not how .nor care,
In millions misbegot.   No power can give
Them wit ; they know not how to live a day.
Their wretched being is a pathless mire,
Wherein the mind lies wallowing evermore.
Their thought, if thought they have, is steeped in vice.
As earthly are their hopes as is the fog
They breathe.   We can, 'tis true, do them no good.
We see them with despair.   Oh, let them die ! "

SATAN.

What means he by this shouting of the truth,
Speaking for others now and not himself ?

DOCTUS.

Is this your proud philosophy, your art
Of words, your science, and your faith ?   To you
Mankind will look in vain for helpful thought.
How can ye justify your deep disgust ?
Man in the mire yet is immortal man,
And claims a brother's care, a brother's aid.
Great men are ye, and, lo, true wisdom lives
With you !   But must it with you die ?   Where then
Is help, and where man's benefactor true ?
Can he be found where men for truth put talk
Of the unknown ; where worship is the sweet
Adoring of Humanity ; where words
Are set for things, and all religion is
Naught but the touch of light and mild constraint
Of poesy ; or, where the word of God

Is made to say what He could never mean ;
Or, where 'tis held man must submit, and serve
The Pope, or see no kingdom of the Lord ?
Ah, no ! What strength to work man's weal has he
That fights the ill with words, however much
They savour of the schools ?   Words are but means
Made vocable by mind.   Can any kill
A vice by praising him that loves the gain
It yields ?   As wise the hope to save the thief
By shewing means of fraud, or poisoned man
By sweet discourse on drugs, or one that reels
Intoxicate by wine.   In vain ye strive,
The heart still unrenewed, to mend the child
Of man, degraded in his sins.   As soon
Will Negro's face look fair as Saxon child.
Begin where He begins who says to all,
" Ye must be born again " ; nor dream that grace
Divine knows but one channel on this earth.
Man's benefactors are the men of faith
Who brace themselves for work, despising shame
And fashion, and behold in every man
A brother whom the love of Christ would save.
With such God works where'er they ply their hands ;
But he that toils to overturn all faith
Is helper to the foes of God and man,
And earns the recompense of deep depair.

SATAN.

I will be gone ; this preaching does me harm ;
But I must wait to see how others judge.

PHANE.

Your doctrine is too positive for me.

HERMES.

We reach by slow degrees what the divines
Set forth as wrought by instant touch of grace.
We mean the same, but our words disagree.

QUAERENS.

I doubted when we met, and still I doubt,
The thought of Richard haunting like a ghost.
To save him from his fate what did his friends?

SATAN.

If it was fate, how could he have been saved?
By turns of thought like this I am relieved.

QUAERENS.

They saw him sink and let him go unwarned.
Thought they no right was theirs to check his course?
Ah, Churchmen might have saved him if they would.

DARDAN.

If you mean Protestants, I disagree.
There is one Church and that is Catholic,

DOCTUS.

And Roman, pagan, sectional, and old,
With incantations most irrational,
Dark practices that shun the light of day,

And a long record of unpardoned crimes.
For doctrines that conceal the cross of Christ,
Making obscure that path which leads to heaven,
When will the Catholic accept the light
Of God, and end the feud between his Church
And truth ?   Till then he knows not perfect peace.

SATAN.

I wish he would not say such rousing things.
Let men alone who know their proper work ;
And, surely, in that Church such men abound.

VICTOR.

We must have facts, or we shall still contend ;
And fighting is the work I can not do.

DOCTUS.

We have more facts than have been fully weighed.
When shall we do our work with honest mind,
And have no ends to serve but ends of truth ?

LUCIDUS.

I too confess ; let me sing you this song
Wherein my ripest thought has found its word :—

> Let them come and let them go ;
> None the mystery can know
>   Of their origin and end.
> We have seen them everywhere,
> Crushed with toil and vexed with care.
>   Who their lot can ever mend ?

Was it God that put them here,
Or did they by chance appear,
   Caused by what the sun might send ?
Evolutions strange have been ;
Such are now in process seen.
   Their own lot they'll never mend.

We have always done our best ;
Now, exhausted, let us rest,
   And to our own good attend ;
Let them spread, and drink, and toil ;
Why should we our fingers soil ?
   We their lot can never mend.

Church they have, and book, and priest,
And might think, say I at least,
   Of the things that upward tend ;
But we have no hope to see
Such wild men with priests agree.
   Creeds their lot will never mend.

We love letters ; they do not ;
What is culture to a sot ?
   Who antipathies can blend ?
One bad case enough for me ;
I have heard, and now I see,
   None their lot can ever mend.

QUAERENS.

To me such words bear no relief. The thought
Is pain, that Richard has been lost. Ah   !

DOCTUS.

Hopeless songs, while men are dying,
   Ill become a bard of light.
Is it sweet, the truth denying,
   To forget the law of right ?
He may sing, and we may listen ;
   What the good of creedless strains ?
When we think, our eyes will glisten
   At the sight of wrongful gains.
Ills abound ; let us redress them.
Men are mourning ; let us bless them.

LUCIDUS.

I know my work, and strive to do it well ;
And men have said so.   Have they said as much
Of hot evangelists whom you would laud ?
I need no such rebuke.   Take your own part ;
And let us see the work which men enjoy.

DOCTUS.

The test is false ; for human praise has oft
Misled the vain ; and He who spake as none
Had ever spoken, met dispraise, and died
Condemned, abhorred, His name cast out by men.
Beware, lest flatt'ry blind you with her lies.

HERMES.

I'll gather facts and ponder more and more,
That I may shew where teachers have gone wrong,
And be a way-mark to the traveller.

ARETAS.

And I will praise the worthy of the race,
Proving the greatness of Humanity,
And be the priest of those who live for man.

DARDAN.

And I must still declare there is one Church,
Wherein the ills of man are all redressed,
And be a prophet in the wilderness.

PHANE.

And I shall mourn the waste of precious time,
Thinking of what we might have done this day,
And be a spur to pierce the sides of sloth.

LUCIDUS.

And I will sing of sweetness and of light,
In hope to reach the dark Philistine horde,
And be a lamp to chase the vulgar gloom.

QUAERENS.

Ye live for reputation and at ease,
While men are wretched at your very doors.

HERMES.

I ne'er have made pretence of Christian life,
But in my solitude have done some work,
To clear the thoughts and ease the load of man ;
And I have prized the function granted me.
Let every worker know what he can do.

There is a life worth living when a man
Has found his place, and toils with all his power,
In Church or State, in letters or in art,
In commerce, or in that delightful field
Of science, where my soul has roamed, by day,
By night, twice twenty years, with joys which words
Can not declare. The life not worth its name
Is the sad life of pleasure, with its haunts
Profane and giddy heartless round of waste
And selfishness. To know your work is done,
Is sweet in life, and should be sweet in death.
But doubt creeps through my nature while I muse.

QUAERENS.

He doeth right who judgeth all the earth,
And faithful souls are lighted with His smile,
For heaven itself is knowledge of His love.

LUCIDUS.

Who cares to know may read, and in my books
Confession find of emptiness and pain.
My hungry soul has ne'er been satisfied,
Though fed with culture, poesy, and fame.
What is it that my nature craves to know ?

QUAERENS.

Who trusts in Christ has everlasting life.
Who serves not Him exists but does not live.

ARETAS.

My satisfaction waits for future years,

When great Humanity, confessed divine,
Shall purge all thought, and beautify all life.
Meanwhile society complains oppressed,
And I live mourning and shall mourning die.
Why am I here to fight the yielding air ?

QUAERENS.

Must I then doubt through all my earthly days,
And find no peace, howe'er I seek or pray ?

DARDAN.

Religion is the culture of the Church,
And Holy Church has met my soul's demand.
She all would pacify, should all obey.
But as a moth a garment gnaws, so doubt
Is eating through her creeds, which soon must fall
To pieces in the hands of men confused
With contradictions vain, but loud, and strong.
There is no life worth living in these days,
And gloomy prospects daily gloomier grow ;
Nor has my work arrested swift decay.

QUAERENS.

Is there, amidst men's interfluent lies,
No central point where truth for ever rests ?

PHANE.

Destruction is sweet work.   The fiends may sneer
While blatant priestly claims are loud, and loud
The boast of science, though, nor here nor there,

Has one man found the rest his nature craves.
My hope is dead. With care I nursed it long,
But saw it dying, and now can not mourn.
I sail serene upon a boundless sea,
Whence, whither, how, be sure, I neither know
Nor wish to learn. Oh, let my being sink
In the abyss, nor found, nor sought, nor missed.

QUAERENS.

My youth is crying for a hand to guide
Across the wild of speculative doubt,
Where ye have roamed without a resting-place.
Has our great King formed us no royal road ?
O Victor, years mature should counsel youth.

VICTOR.

My age is full, but youth may counsel years.
How I once hungered for the truth you name,
Hopefully seeking where I seek not now !
I walked with bards and loved their songs inspired,
And books went with me as the friend in need,
While music me entranced, and gave my soul
Glimpse of the infinite, through thought of God
And heaven. Where now the mystic pulse of sound,
And where the mast'ry of inventive mind,
The charms of poesy and rapturous song ?
Do any feel to-day what then I felt,
Admiring legends of the lyre divine,
Whose notes bade beasts applaud and woods attend ?
In art I revelled, through my buoyant youth.

The sculptured form, which wanted only breath,
And painted guise of beauty, gave my soul
Delight.   Then earth a symbol was of heaven,
And man the image of his God, but naught
That knowledge which could shew no way to Him.

   Ah, how I wonder that I ever prayed,
Upon my knees before the great Unknown !
What then I saw, Quaerens, I see no more ;
Naught is discerned of what I deemed divine.
O could I now as then, my eyelids closed,
Look up afar !   But other thoughts have sway ;
And through my being creeps the chill of doubt.
My old belief lies dead, or sleeps, no more
To wake, which is the same.   Without a sigh
It sank to perfect rest, one limb entire
Of my strange manhood lost.   What has been killed ?
Oh, am I guiltless where guilt brings dismay,
Before that bar of which my teachers spake,
When I was taught God ruleth over all ?

   Why am I thus bereft of what I prized ?
O'er this, 'tis wonderful, I can not mourn !
Slowly I found a perfect anodyne,
Nor heart nor conscience craving more to find.
I do not know, is what we say in books ;
I do not care, is what we say at home ;
Yet live I not in perfect calm of mind.
Maimed as I am and must, I ween, remain,
I feel my want and imperfection.   None
Need tell me I have lost part of myself.
I know it, and must blame my own neglect.

O had I weekly tuned my failing ear,
And checked the atrophy I now record,
By contact with the great in art and song !
What can it profit me to have disclosed
The origin of species, at the price
Of losing from myself what once I most
Esteemed ?   What now for me can raise the dead,
Restoring my lost love of letters, art,
And song, to make me just myself again ?
I wander on and grope, uncertain still,
And to my cry there comes no clear response,
If 'tis a cry my nature utters now.
A feat has been achieved, and I am spent ;
But men will speak my name from age to age.
Oh, how I wish my days could be prolonged !
Then would I teach what man has never known.

   My shrinking frame is sliding to the grave ;
This eye grows dim ; but through my nerves a mind
Is quiv'ring still in undecaying power.
I dream that souls are naught but transient breath,
And soon I must on earth be but a name.
Meanwhile I know no rest, no holiday,
My pleasure work, my joy colossal toil,
Which much will leave how hopelessly obscure !
Who will arise to fill my vacant place,
Who to correct the error of my thought,
To demonstrate what I have but surmised,
And make complete the work by me begun ?
Faith has its load to bear, and this no-faith
Is burdened too.   O friend, which fares the worse ?

Calmly I lost the burden of the creed,
And took instead the load of no-belief,
Which now is crushing and may crush me more.
  The dream is vanishing.   This land of shades
Will soon be lost to sight.   Where shall I sail
In the immense ?   Ah, shall I sail at all ?
'Tis thought the dead, unseen, their course pursue.
Why comes the ancient faith to mock me now ?
The darkest clouds are mists and fogs of doubt.
In clouds I live, and I in clouds may die !
But I in death shall feel no fear, no joy.
Who, who the deep uncertainty shall clear ?

QUAERENS.

What food for hunger is vast emptiness !
My life is strangled in this noisome air.
Let me go forth to think of God and heaven,
And find my bliss in order and in faith.

HERMES.

What is this Victor says of a light he has lost ?
  He forgets all has changed in his time.
'Tis not well that his mind should in this way be tossed,
  As if all had gone wrong since his prime.
Side by side have we worked in the days that are past,
  And I trust we are far from the end,
But so sensible am I that things can not last,
  And so little know whither I tend,
That I start at the sight of my wrinkles and gray,
  And grow anxious as though a divine

Had been preaching to lead me to follow his way,
    And abandon all hitherto mine.
I have loved letters well, and the great, in their books,
    My best friends and companions have been,
But their errors I've tracked into corners and nooks,
    For my eye has them evermore seen.
You may ask what is gained by such merciless rout,
    And I answer, with pain of the mind,
It has left me to sink in a fathomless doubt,
    And no certainly ever to find.
I have fought, and will fight, in the cause of the truth,
    And at last I my pæan will sing,
Though now lost many hopes which I cherished in youth
    Of the blessing that science should bring.
That perverse human nature which baffles my schemes
    Has exhausted the patience I had ;
For the priests and the parsons, great dreamers of dreams,
    By opacity drive a man mad.
Now corrected they stand, as they well have deserved,
    And will shrink at the sound of my name.
Do you see that in this a good cause has been served,
    Or behold but a glittering game ?
Men have thought me severe in my critical fence
    And have censured my methods and aims ;
But vexation has nerved me, and my recompense
    Is a power which my enemies shames.
Though my life is declining and soon will have gone
    To the dust and the darkness of death,
Yet that intellect which in my writings has shone
    Still must shine when has vanished my breath.

'Tis a comfort to me that the form of my face
    Men will study for many a day ;
Yet immortal I am not except in the race,
    But must totally sink in decay.

QUAERENS.

Oh, vanity of empty fame !
    How great in one that thinks,
Soon as the breath has left the frame
    To naught man's being sinks.
If spirits share the frame's decay,
    Expiring with the breath,
And naught in man shall bloom for aye,
    Defying pain and death,
How great the vanity of those
    Whom Hermes typifies !
They fill their life to its sad close
    With hopes that are but lies.

SATAN.

Let them go ; where'er they wend,
Trouble they will never end.
Long ere manhood reached its noon,
Light they had, Heaven's richest boon.
But they would not use their sight,
Nor retain it when they might.
I was near them in their pride,
From them striving not to hide
What, I knew, must work their fall.
Of themselves they gave up all

That they ever had believed.
Then the light by faith received
Left the souls that would not seek,
In the spirit of the meek,
That sure sense of things divine
Which sets man above the swine.
Eyes they had, but would not see ;
Now, grown blind, they grope to me.

   Spreads my conquest more and more ;
I shall reign on every shore.
What can now my sway confine,
Since the knowing ones are mine ?
Me it pleases well to see
How such potent souls agree
In rejecting all the creeds,
Which, to serve me, no one needs.
Strange that sages bear such strife
'Twixt the conscience and the life !

   Man on earth is sorrow's heir ;
Boasting is no cure for care ;
And these sages can but sigh,
Knowing not their tears to dry,
When, in crowd or solitude,
Deep they feel their nature's feud.
Know they what the feud portends ?
They will know when gained my ends,
If they reach the pathless sea
On which many come to me,
Who have all their voyage seen,
  And their watchful captain been.

On the strand the wreckage strewn
Tells of those who light had known,
But, bewildered, lost their way,
And for ever left the day.
Who will sink as sinks the barque
Wrecked in midnight starless dark,
Mourning that fell power which rules
Wasted lives of learned fools ?

What though mighty thinkers keen
Leave memorials to be seen,
If they pass to sail with me
On the boundless pathless sea
Where eternal tempests roll
That can never drown a soul ?
Restless, lightless, hopeless fate,
Produce of Satanic hate
For the word in mercy given
To make plain the path to heaven !

XIV.—ST. BARTHOLOMEW'S HOSPITAL.

A true physician of the mind
Is he who, God's own truth to find,
  Ponders the written word,
And tenderly to souls in pain,
And gently as distils the rain,
  Imparts what he has heard.

The body's good physician he
To whom true science gives to see
  Man's nature, state, and need,
And who, with freedom, faith, and skill,
And firmness of a practised will,
  Doth weakness wisely lead.

Agnoscens dreams; and by a bed,
While whispering nurses lightly tread,
  He sits to watch and learn.
The voice of one that nears the grave
Tells him how fully Christ can save,
  And faith its heaven discern.

---

*Stephanas. A House Surgeon. A Medical Student.
Nurses. Patients.*

HOUSE SURGEON.

Yes, Stephanas is going. Well I knew
He could not live for many weeks when first

I diagnosed the case ; and you will see
Confirmed my diagnosis in each part.
I hope, when we examine after death,
You will attend.   The case will shew you much.
I like a case with features strong.

MEDICAL STUDENT.

I know
This patient is remarkable for more
Than you have named.   I like the man.

HOUSE SURGEON.

I think
The hist'ry of the case is worth a word.
The man was here some months ago and left
Restored, we thought ; but in his system lay
Concealed what now must bring him to the grave.
The body's a great myst'ry to us all.

MEDICAL STUDENT.

He suffers much ; but have you marked the calm
Of his repose ?

HOUSE SURGEON.

Oh, yes, his temperament
Is of the gentlest sort, as soft as cream.
I like that better than the surly kind.
The other week we had a man who cursed,
And looked most vicious, when a paroxysm
Came on him.   This man lives at an extreme
Quite opposite.   Let nature have her way.

MEDICAL STUDENT.

I see in him what you have not explained.
The calmness of his soul is, I believe,
The fruit of grace divine, implored in prayer,
And granted to that faith which rests in Christ.

HOUSE SURGEON.

I find no meaning in the words you say.
My explanation takes another form,
And you may live to see that I am right.
Let us together go and note the case.
One minute will suffice for what I want.
I can not stay.

MEDICAL STUDENT.

The man has much to tell,
Not many words, but much in every one.
You'll hear him speak of dying, with no fear.
His words have come to me with wondrous power,
And his bright life will have triumphant end.

HOUSE SURGEON.

You talk of what I can not understand.
Triumph belongs to that fell tyrant, death.

STEPHANAS.

I knew, long before
I came by that door,
The secret of peace,
And hoped for release.

N

O doctor, I lie,
Made ready to die.
The Saviour of all
Hears me when I call.

HOUSE SURGEON.

What science can do
Have we done for you,
To lessen your pain
And life to sustain.

STEPHANAS.

And now I must wait
  The bidding divine,
To change my estate ;
  But Jesus is mine.
My ailments do grow ;
I surely must go.

MEDICAL STUDENT.

I see in your face
The tokens of grace,
As peaceful you lie,
No tear in your eye.

STEPHANAS.

Lord, mighty to save,
Though death and the grave
Before me appear,
To fill me with fear,

I victory see
Assured unto me,
While here I remain,
In weakness and pain,
To Thee yielded up,
Who minglest my cup.

MEDICAL STUDENT.

And when to the skies
Your soul shall arise,
Forsaking the clay
Which shrinks in decay
At the portals of bliss,
True rapture is this,
The Saviour to love,
With pure ones above,
Fulfil His behest,
Eternally blessed
With the smile that is heaven.
    Then why are we given
To weeping and grief
When those gain relief
Who walked with us here ?
It doth not appear
What they have to be,
Or what they will see,
Who die in the Lord ;
But this in the word
We clearly discern
And joyfully learn :

All trial is o'er,
And saints evermore
Will serve God in light
Not followed by night.

NURSE.

Infirmity quails
When Satan assails
Those who can but mourn,
By conscience o'erborne ;
And oft have I seen
Their anguish, how keen !
But Stephanas waits
At the open gates
Of heaven, in peace
Which never shall cease.

STEPHANAS.

I will not complain
Of weakness and pain ;
Ah, no ; but I fain,—

MEDICAL STUDENT.

Will welcome the fight
To the home of delight,
The face to behold
Of Him who was sold
To die on the cross
The infinite loss
Of man to retrieve.

STEPHANAS.

In Him I believe ;
And He draweth near,
And saveth from fear.

NURSE.

The sight of His face
All sorrow shall chase ;
And when at His feet
The faithful you meet,
Your service will be
For eternity.
But now you must rest.

*   *   *

Recline on my breast.

*   *   *

He sleeps and may not wake again.

A PATIENT.

I knew him in his early days
When he by grace took Christian ways.
How patiently he bears his pain !

MEDICAL STUDENT.

By grace he has a soaring mind ;
To what he sees most men are blind.
How sweet the strain in which he spoke,
Not fearing death's most awful stroke.
If I may watch his dying breath,
I shall be helped to think of death

Without dismay.

STEPHANAS.

He speaks to me.

NURSE.

He sees a light we do not see,
And hears a voice we do not hear.
The gate of heaven to us how near !

*   *   *

STEPHANAS.

My days of grief and pain are past,
And I have victory at last.
No foe molests, I feel no shock,
My feet now standing on the rock.
I come, O Lord, to obey Thy call,
And on Thy mercy cast my all.

*   *   *

NURSE.
He dies to live, and sinks to rise.
  Ah, he has passed the mystic way,
And opens now adoring eyes,
  In the eternal tearless day.
Saw ye the light which from him shone
Just as we thought his spirit gone ?
It streamed as rose his new-found wing
On flight for home.   There will he sing
  The victor's song,

And joy prolong
  For evermore.
    On yonder shore
Meet all that loved the Lord on earth,
And died, but dying found a birth
  To richer life.
    Nor pain nor strife
Can e'er be known in that fair land.
I wonder how upon the strand
  That skirts the sea of death,
    And knows no mortal breath,
The saints of God their powers employ,
And find expression for their joy.
O may I wait in patience still,
Gladly to do my Master's will.
So shall I know as I am known
Standing before the eternal throne.

A PATIENT.

Mature in him was Christian grace,
And heaven has touched his resting-place.

ANOTHER PATIENT.

How much is done for that poor cheat ;
Let death the hypocrite defeat.
'Tis easy when a man expires
To think him breathing good desires.
This ward's a church, I do believe,
  Where only pious ones receive

Attention suited to our need.
I'm sure the Sisters have been feed.

PATIENTS.

Shame, shame ! Impossible !

NURSE.

Alas,
That one could think that Stephanas
Could be a hypocrite in death,
And utter lies with his last breath.
He was a lover of the truth,
And walked in virtue from his youth.
The counsels of his soul were sweet,
And he through grace for heaven was meet.

ANOTHER NURSE.

Yes, Stephanas obeyed his guide,
　　Christ, all in all !
A door for him set open wide,
　　He heard a call,
And stood before the Saviour's face,
To serve Him, in the holy place,
Witness for ever of His grace.

We went with him and reached the door,
　　But saw not through.
He passed, and it was closed, before
　　We aught could do.
We might not instantly withdraw,

But stood a while in wondering awe ;
And naught but saintliness we saw.

He dewed his path with many a tear,
    For others shed,
Who walked in sorrow, doubt, or fear.
    Can he be dead
Whose passing was a sweet release,
A stepping iuto perfect peace,
Wherein all bliss must now increase ?

Welcome to him the grace divine !
    The holy way
In which his footsteps brightly shine
    Invites to-day.
This treasure now is all our own,
A spotless pattern meekly shewn,
For we a saint on earth have known.

       *   *   *

HOUSE SURGEON.

They say that Stephanas has gone. I knew
He could not last when first I saw the case.
At the *post-mortem*, you will surely find
My diagnosis quite confirmed. To me
A case like this is full of interest,
And I will shew you where its value lies.

NEW NURSE.

Is this a horse-doctor ? He ought to be.
It makes me shudder when I hear him talk
About the case. But he is learned. Ah !
Well, I have heard that science does not feel.

NURSE.

We must have charity and patience too.
Come now with me ; our work is done. The men
Will bear this body to its destined place,
And there the surgeon will discourse, to suit
Himself, and prove or find disproved his view
Of the disease.   Oh, Stephanas is gone !

NEW NURSE.

The man is most hard-hearted.

NURSE.

You misjudge.

He's not hard-hearted, but a constant use
Has brought a second nature, and he sees
With scientific eyes in every case.

*　　　*　　　*　　　*

HOUSE SURGEON.

Well now, my diagnosis was confirmed.
That case must be reported in the press.
I'll write myself.

MEDICAL STUDENT.

And there is much to say.

I wish we could report the faith that shone
And glowed in Stephanas in life and death.

HOUSE SURGEON.

He was a meek and gentle man, andbore
His lot most bravely, for he was mild-born.

MEDICAL STUDENT.

Nay ; meekness was a gift of grace, sought long
In faith from God who made his nature new.
Those who have known him best have loved him most.

XV.—TARTARUS.

———

Agnoscens dreams that in the deep
Where spirits dwell, and long for sleep
  But long in vain, he visits men,
    And hears them speak :
    " When shall we rest," they cry, " Oh, when ?
Comes there no calm to conscience-storm,
No beauty to one spirit-form
    Howe'er we seek ? "
Agnoscens, dreaming, wonders more !
He sees a sea without a shore,
  And hears a ceaseless tempest rave,
    And lists the moan,
    " There is no hand from wrath to save
Spirits o'erwhelmed through vain deceit,
Who light called dark and bitter sweet,
    And now but groan."

———

Arouet. Historicus. Pannus. Audax. Richard. Satan.

SATAN.

My rage is full, and I have come in haste,
For sages have confessed their emptiness,
And great ones have been humbled to the dust,
And youth has baffled age.   Yet in a house

Made famous by the learning honoured there,
I heard my servants boast of what I like.
But, Oh, the Nazarene is prosp'ring still.

AROUET.

Amazing that they see it not ! We tried ·
The sages' plan in France, in that bright day
When I was king of letters, and gave laws
To men and women, and withstood the Church.
My work was never finished. When I came
Below it languished ; but it still has life ;
And we shall hear all Europe knows Voltaire,
Though I am known below by my true name.

HISTORICUS.

In fair Britannia's isle the plan was tried,
In boldest form, when I would undermine
The ground on which the Church is built, the deep
Rock fundamental, miracles. My wit,
By all confessed, made many quail ; and skill
Immense and loads of lore were spent on me,
To drive me off, my work still incomplete.
That work was done with care, and brought me fame,
And my escutcheon still is bright on earth ;
But honour can not breathe this nether air,
And what I deemed a gain has proved a loss.

PANNUS.

I on two continents, in that bold work
Of sweet destruction, took my faithful part,
But fared no better than the great had fared

Before me.　I was lithe in all my work,
And many changes saw, but through them all
Persistently withstood the Nazarene.
What now the profit of my boastful noise
And homage of the cringing populace ?
My glory sinks in night which knows no morn.

AUDAX.

I tried the plan, struck hard, and failed, in times
More recent, when the voice of science, heard
In every land, proclaimed as near the end
Of all theology and Christian faith.
I saw not then, as I have seen below,
How palsied falls the arm that fights the truth.

RICHARD.

Ye are philosophers of other days,
Of whom I scarce have heard on earth above ;
But ye resemble men to me well known
Who flourish now, if thus I say the truth
Speaking of those who have to me been guides.
　One deeply mourns his loss of early love,
By science robbed, and doubts if he is wise,
Life's evening shadows falling on his brow,
And the dark tomb awaiting his descent.
A little while will make him wise as we.
　One, light to spread, brings forth a gloomy book,
And thinks he teaches when he but obscures
By words magniloquent in sound, not sense ;
But he destroys the faith his mother taught,

And mocks with want the souls that cry for bread.
By aid of death he will again believe.

    Another seems to worship man, and talks,
As if he had a faith, of views and aims
Humanitarian, but finds and must
Confess his god impure.   He can not pray.
A child may shew the folly of his creed.
Ah, he may learn when learning comes too late.

    Another owns no trust in God, in man,
In aught, and would destroy all faith confessed
In letters, art, or work, or song.   Alas,
His doubt of all things pleased myself too well.
He will believe if he descend below ;
And I may taunt him with discipleship.

    Another has grown sure that on the earth
Life is not worth the living, since the Pope
No longer holds the intellect in chains,
Where contradiction rends the air.   Ah me !
So thought I once, and madly left my place
Before the time, and came surprised to you.

    My darkening life was better than my death,
Which was not worth the dying ; but too late
I knew my folly.   I wish I could warn
Such as now follow those who hither led
My willing feet.   Oh, how I scorn their names,
Knowing they can not thwart the Nazarene,
But must o'erthrow themselves, and rue like me.

AUDAX.

'Tis not for man to thwart the Nazarene,

Who prospers as appointed King of all.
I knew not this above, but thought I proved
He could not gain His end.   Alas, too hot
My feverish hate to let me live !   It burned
The spirit's house of flesh while life was young,
And my great work in but dim prospect seen.
I fell asone that puts his armour on
But lives not to assay it in the field.
I reap the harvest that my sin has sown,
And still blaspheme and curse the light of truth,
Which shines no less for all the hate, the rage,
That withered my keen soul as an east wind,
While passion tortured with acutest pain.
I heard the voice of God, (but would not heed,)
Which echoed through the caverns of old time,
And echoes still in my tumultuous soul.
Ah, shall I hear it to eternity ?
Thus will my being laugh itself to scorn
Amidst the quenchless fires men call remorse.

RICHARD.

Is there no hope, and must all wishing cease ?
Is this the price of that mean fleeting good
Which me deceived in living for the flesh ?
My frame is left behind to feed the worms,
Not sharing now my consciousness and woe.

AUDAX.

We are alike.   I can not comfort thee.
None comforts me.   There is no comfort here.

Over the past quick memory daily runs,
Returning home with whips that strike
And swords that pierce, to give us ceaseless pain.
We still rebel and sin, while dread, rage, woe
Make agony beyond the power of words.
We reap as we have sown, and thou wilt learn.

AROUET.

Long lives the conflict with the powers of hell.
I left them winning when I came below,
But now they fail because they have no guide
Like me.   'Tis pain to know the Nazarene,
In might enthroned, is Conqueror.   My load
Becomes too heavy to be borne, my fame
Lying in dust, and my predictions bold
All falsified, though still read in my books,
Whereby, in thought, I chased all godliness.
How have I failed !

PANNUS.

                The times have widely changed.
Blaspheming men, so called by those who fought
For creeds, were many in my day.   Where now
Are they whose antichristian zeal led hosts
Against the Lord ?   To overthrow the King
How have they failed ! They spake, as I, of rights
And wrongs, and called eternal vengeance down
On all oppressive laws and men who them
Enacted.   What reward ?   I see around
The victims of deceptive love of self,

o

Of place, of power, and am dismayed to know
My being an unceasing stream of ill.
The rights of man I never knew above.
But in an age when reason was eclipsed,
I followed fatuous guides, and led astray
Who went with me, nor sought the light of heaven.
Ages have rolled, and I am wretched still.
Yea, wretchedness is now my bread of life,
And I, subdued, am prostrate in this woe.

HISTORICUS.

I proudly made strong work for men of might,
As all confessed. Great was my joy, my glee,
When I beheld their struggles. I esteemed
The truth of God no stronger than its friends.
That truth, which metaphysic strife a while
Obscured, now shines on me, and evermore
I mourn my folly irreversible,
And curse the beams that shew me to myself,
And curse the day when I was born, and curse
You all. Yet cursing is a work I hate.
But hate and cursing are my fellows here.

AROUET.

My power confessed on earth by mortal man,
What gain I with this retrospect of woe ?
O that yon gate were closed against mankind !
When they whom I have taught to curse come down,
My burden grows, and I, the wretch, am crushed.
Frivolity, and foolishness, and scorn

Served for an hour a purpose strong but mean,
And I am mocked in reaping what I sowed,
Hope, peace, and love denied me evermore.
I hear mad laughter of disdainful minds,
I see the sneer of scorn on many a face,
I feel the gnawings of my conscience-worm,
And well I know Jehovah keeps His word ;
And I am conquered by the Nazarene.
If I had lived in prayer and done His will,
Then had my journey ended in His heaven.

RICHARD.

'Tis strange to me to hear these worded sighs,
These groans articulate.   How impotent
Your vengeance, and how heartless the vain boast
That ye interpret man's dark history.
Your sun has set and can no more arise.

AROUET.

Thou wilt learn something by abiding here.

HISTORICUS.

And here he must abide, whate'er his will.
Our being is abiding without end.
O that destroyed we might abide no more !

AUDAX.

Here is no calm for any soul oppressed,
But sleepless introspection is our work,

And from ourselves we naught bring forth of good.
Our being is the mockery of lies.

PANNUS.

And hatred is the element, wherein
We plan, and plan, and plan ;

AROUET.

                And wait, and wait,
And wait to execute the plan, and wait
And plan again, and wait, and wait, and wait,
Nor peace nor patience granted with our pain.
For us has ceased to roll the wheel of time.
Eternity is centred in this now,
And being is endurance without end,
No ray of hope illumining the gloom.
Our plenteous sowing yields abundantly
On earth and here. O mystery of lies !
The past remains and grows, and on it rests
Eternal judgment. Oh, how long ? We plan
And wait, and plan and wait, cursing and cursed.
O could we vanish into nothingness !
Who then to reap the harvest we have sown,
Maintain the balance of man's destiny,
And feel Jehovah keeps His sacred word ?
O Richard, know the lot thou hast to share.

RICHARD.

I stand in my own place, a suicide,
Amazed to share your lot, deceived, betrayed

By lies that smiled upon my wantonness.
Then was I bold, defiant, and profane,
And thought my licence could not see an end.
But on me now is an abiding chain,
And I am hopeless in this realm of sighs,
My being blighted for eternity,
Where none can help, none pity, none relieve.
My guides I blame, but am my own worst foe,
Since I had light and would not walk therein.

SATAN.

Ye men of intellect who shook the world,
What had ye been without my art, my aid,
And what achieved ?   I was your constant guide,
And fed from day to day the fires that burned
In you, though ye denied and would not own
My rule.   The end is gained, and I rejoice,
In that dread sense in which, accursed, I can.
But I am hindered in the fight severe,
Because my strategy is known and checked.
Those whom ye left shall have my help.   They hold
Delusive lights before the wand'rer's eye,
By me employed, they see not how nor care.
Your day has gone, and ye can aid no more ;
But your defiant thought is yet alive
In mystic force, and throbs through Christendom.
Your books are read as generations come
And go ; they nourish pride by vain conceits.
Thus is your fame defying time a while.
But it will die, as ye have died, and live,

As ye live here, in righteous recompense.
But wherefore speak I thus to you, defied ?
Because ye were confederate with me
In my great work, and share my hopeless gloom.
Welcome are ye to all that I can give,
Since ye are fit to dwell with me below,
Partakers of the lot for me prepared.
Fitness is Heaven's eternal changeless law.
Oh, to endure in chains which me defy,
Provoke, and madden !   But my work remains
And prospers.   Still I goad, I taunt, I mock
The victims of deception, who, to please
Themselves, withstand the truth and hate the light;
And ye had part in this my happiness,
Such happiness as souls destroyed can feel.
   Rejoice with me, as fiends rejoice, ye men
Of intellectual might, who led the hosts
That poured through Christendom a stream of fire,
When thrice six ages had their cycles run
Since Christ appeared, the light of all the world.
While terror reigned, the curse that rests on me
Seemed lighter ; but my desp'rate aim was foiled,
Though much was planned and done.   A noble state,
Torn as a mountain from its ancient seat,
Was hurled by me to crush all Christian power,
And much was killed of what my nature hates.
But here and there survived a witness strong,
Whom God empowered to work my overthrow
With Heaven's mysterious truth, which I abhor.
I am defeated in my realm usurped,

But still my zeal, uncooled, burns and will burn,
And know no mitigation of its rage,
Howe'er the Conqueror crush my rebel soul.

   Ye help no more ; yet I am not alone,
But strong in aid of those who proudly boast
Of zeal to serve their fellow men, and think
They know. Ah, such despise the peerless name
Of Him who blessed the meek, and promised sight
To hearts of truth alone. Well they serve me,
The foe (through my short day) of love and strength,
Of purity, of God, and of His Christ ;
And they uphold my tottering reign of wrong.

   Ye who, in active war, stood with me once,
Can never rest, though now ye fight no more.
This pathless sea of gloom is mine and yours ;
Be welcome to a share of agony.
To do my will, has been to curse yourselves,
And being now is but a crushing load,
Which will, as cycles roll, too heavy grow.
The worlds are old, and each is in decay.
All must erelong renew their mighty youth.
O that with them my being were consumed,
And thought were ended in forgetfulness ;
But hope is not that God will grant the boon.

   Upon this pathless sea of boundless woe,
Far have we floated from the central sun,
Yet memory links us to the Father's throne
Whose glory, glimpsing, never can be hid.

   Behold you beauteous star, now twinkling sole
Athwart this nether gloom. Ye see the light

Of heaven, distant but clear. Naught can be seen
Except its beauty. It will never cease
On you to shine, revealing, by its light,
No path, no hope, no touch of blessedness,
Naught but itself, nor that for us. It is
Our central sun ; but we, cast out the realm
Of life beyond, here die the second death,
And float away past all the bounds of thought,
For ever lost, but kept in sight of heaven.

    How will ye bear to see that taunting light ?
My pleasure is, to know ye gaze intent
Upon the lustrous world of peace and joy,
And hear you vainly wish, and curse yourselves,
And life, and time, and earth, and heaven, and hell,
And that pure rule which binds you to your fate.
Cursing but gnaws the restless impious soul.
Curse on, and ye shall smart the more. Curse on,
Curse on, and yonder sphere shall mock your woe,
And wormwood shall be all your daily fare,
And converse shall increase its bitterness ;
While those who come to join you shall but curse ;
And I will sneer, as none but Satan can,
To mock your aggravated woe. Ah me,
Our sighs are heard afar ; but were their sound
To travel through the universe of worlds,
It would not touch the atmosphere of heaven,
Wherein the saints of God live evermore,
In plenitude of bliss by love bestowed,
Their temple, the new earth, to us unseen.

XVI.—PARADISE.

Change infinite ! Agnoscens thinks,
  Upheld by God's almighty grace,
  He traverses the interspace,
And from the fount eternal drinks.

Then, standing on the mount of song,
  He hears the saints their worship give
  To Him in whom they move and live,
And marvels they this strain prolong :—

" No rest these spotless spirits crave ;
  Active is being in this light,
  Advancing on perfection's height,
Through Him who died our souls to save."

*Pascal. Kempis. Luther. Epicus. Edwards. Butler.
Musicus. Channing. Meditans. Firmus. Stephanas.*

STEPHANAS.

Where am I now, and where are they
  Who watched in love my bed of death ?
They prayed that I, throughout the way
  Entered as ceased my labouring breath,
Might go in light.   It hath been so !
  But where am I, and where are they ?

I see them not, nor saw them go ;
    Nor have I found this peerless day
One cause of fear, one anxious thought.
    A lowly place contents me here,
Beyond the reach of sorrow brought.
    The sights, the sounds, the work make clear
This is the home of saints !   They wait
    Till He who saved them by His grace
Shall come again in pomp of state,
    While nature shrinks before His face,
To open heaven to all His own
    And crown them with eternal fame.
I marvel most to me was shewn
    The path whereby the pure ones came

FIRMUS.

One whom I knew, saved from the strife of earth !
He walked in virtue, and has passed in peace ;
We welcome him, born into paradise ;
And he will learn, untaught, our rapturous songs.

CHANNING.

The air of this good land is fragrant truth,
The element wherein we live.   On earth
We knew a little and esteemed it much,
Our error pardoned for the love we had.
Great was and is the mercy of our God.
This new-born friend will learn by living here,
And find no limit to his nature's growth.

EDWARDS.

Our dialectic skill was blind in part,
Nor found at times the home of sweetened thought,
Where dwelt the souls suffused with sympathy,
Whose learning was the love of God and man.
We erring groped, but were in love restrained.
How we can think amidst the light of heaven
Where error can not be ! Great love of God !

BUTLER.

How contrary was man ! He saw the good
And yet the ill pursued, and craved his woe,
An enemy perverting his intent.
But in this land of light truth is supreme,
And folly has no place. Order is love,
While all obey one common sweet constraint
To grow in good, as once on earth they breathed.
We who then but opined now clearly see.

STEPHANAS.

What is the strain I hear ? 'Tis new, yet seems
It old. To me on earth in solitude
Once came, as borne upon the passing breeze,
Some wondrous notes that live in memory still.
They were a part of this world's rapturous song,
By angel-touch conveyed from paradise ;
And I have come to find what then I hoped.
The minstrelsy of heaven tunes my deep soul,
And I of rapture taste initial share,
Waiting the fulness of my bliss to know.

MUSICUS.

We sang as sing the birds by nature moved,
In forest trees, when genial rays of spring
Renew the glow of love. We rose at times
On venturous wing to feel the touch of heaven
While genius breathed of mystery the air.
Yet then our anthems were but prophecy
Of that sweet play of reason, grace, and love,
Which is the music of this holy land.
We sing with majesty as roll the worlds,
Our songs in time, in tune, with their great march.
We sing Messiah who has freed the hosts
Of faith from every foe, and led to bliss
Supreme ; and angels join the symphony
Divine, nor find it such as bore the taint
Of earthly minds. The music of this land
Is truth ; and all can sing, and singing serve.
'Twas not in vain we tuned our notes below,
And caught faint echoes of the perfect strain,
For we have risen to wonder and adore.

EPICUS.

The harps of earth were lent to us by Heaven,
And o'er them breathed a minstrelsy divine ;
But feeble were the harpers, and failed oft
To honour truth. Yet when we sang that love
Which man redeemed and led in all his ways,
The angels listened, as they listen now,
To catch the highest strain in worship used
In all the universe. To us, redeemed,

Is given this work supreme, to sing as sang
The morning stars when all was good ; for we
The new creation sing and paradise
Regained by Him who gave His life for vast
Mankind, and lives by all the saints adored.

MEDITANS.

The saints of God dwell here in light,
And fill with praise heaven's echoing height ;
For paradise, through all her fields,
To holy spirits rapture yields.

Only a while this home is ours ;
For soon will sound through all its bowers
The word, " Arise ; with me to earth ;
I give your bodies second birth."

Immortal then our spotless dress ;
Our bodies, raised for blessedness,
Shall make complete that good estate,
That bliss supreme, for which we wait.

Meanwhile, in all our being blessed,
Active, we find our perfect rest.
This service is free nature's play,
And naught can e'er our progress stay.

STEPHANAS.

Ah, when the strains I hear
Which come near and more near,
My nature prompt replies,
That ere I scaled the skies,

Leaving the earth,
My place of birth,
Some fore-notes fell upon my soul,
And me enraptured past control.
Then as I came above,
Upborne on wings of love,
Those fore-notes ceasèd not but grew.
When past the worlds which star-deeps strew
I took my way,
(My path the day,)
The fore-notes swelled.   Now here
I shall with those appear
Who join to sing
My Saviour-King,
By whose pure grace
I have a place
Among the saints that serve for aye
In heaven's serene eternal day.

PASCAL.

In Church and State abuses spread, and called
For pruning, but the knife was held by few,
Though many poured complaint.   Our witness still
We bore, nor were dismayed, though anger, scorn,
And ribaldry assailed.   Where we had looked
For love and purity, spread rank offence,
And stern rebuke, how needful ! soon was heard,
A lesson taught for every future age.
But, Oh, the creature, waiting, hath not ceased
To groan, so calling on the Lord.

LUTHER.

                    The truth,
So long obscured, came into view at length
Through toil. The curse of power rang o'er the realm.
We fought, we won the day, nor love was lost
Amidst the strife, wisdom divine our guide.

MEDITANS.

The day was won, and love was saved to weep
Because the truth, checked by unrighteousness,
Was known and not obeyed. God sent a voice
Which called a slumb'ring nation and was heard ;
And mercy through that nation taught the world,
As decades rolled and evangelic zeal
Burned off the bonds of Churches old and young,
In east, and west, and north, and south. But still
Worked on the ancient mystery of sin,
And priestly folly reimposed the bonds
In Anglia's favoured land, where liberty,
We hoped, would live and grow until the end.
O'er the enslaved now weeps the friend of truth,
Nor doubts God's purpose yet shall be revealed,
All folly banished to its own abode.

KEMPIS.

The joy which is in Christ for all the true,
Who Him obey, was known in common walks
Of care ; and then, the Pattern understood,
Earth grew like heaven in lives of lowly love,
True witness of that law of grace which sin

To shame condemned.   Society decayed
Where that true witness failed ; but where, as salt
Arrested swift decay, the witness checked
The course of ill, there flourished all the fruits
Of peace, to comfort those who mourned for sin
And sought in Christ the light of heavenly truth,
Renouncing all the vanities of sense,
And pleasures which allured to foolishness.

FIRMUS.

I came but lately to this realm of joy,
And to my memory clings, not giving pain,
The cry that swells from earth to heaven.   It is
A cry of sin, of shame, of woe, and calls
For punishment severe.   Dark crime
Abounds, and conflict rends the air, the wit
And strength of man perverted to worst ends.
Satan is still obeyed and feared by men,
Though known as tyrant and usurper both ;
And subtlest means of ill are promptly plied.
But we are saved, and have not toiled in vain.

CHANNING.

Through purest mercy have we all been saved,
Redeemed with blood, though once we knew it not.

MEDITANS.

We stand upon the verge of time to watch,
As come and go successors of our race,
Who fill their days and pass to destiny.

The mystery of God will be complete ;
But for a while we wait, adore, and serve,
Saved from the errors that were clouds of mind
While we pursued on earth our chosen ways.

FIRMUS.

Some walked in error as their path elect,
Not loving truth when known, yea, deeply felt
In keen conviction.   How they wronged themselves
In falsehood, malice, fraud, and strenuous war
Of sin with purity, where more than blood
Was shed.   In that stupendous strife I took
My part, before I came above and left
My weapons, needed then no more ; but here
The power that wielded them shall serve the Lord
In ways which filial love will find and prize.

KEMPIS.

We who on earth welcomed the dawn of truth
Now see the day, and wait the full reward,
A grand apocalypse, which draweth nigh.
Then shall our soaring thought its fulness reach,
Spirit and body in beatitude,
The latest foe by power divine destroyed.

MEDITANS.

Meanwhile we wait in purest joy,
Since every power hath sweet employ.

PASCAL.

Yea, we the perfect good have found ;
And depth and height with praise resound.

MEDITANS.

We wonder that, in mercy brought,
We have the good for which we sought ;

CHANNING.

And wonder most at that pure grace
Which shewed us the Redeemer's face ;

BUTLER.

And glory in the light that shone,
To bid our doubts and fears be gone ;

EDWARDS.

And bade our powers the Lord adore,
Devoted to him evermore.

KEMPIS.

The Pattern followed led us hither,
Where no delight can ever wither.

FIRMUS.

We fought, we conquered in the strife,
Our great reward eternal life.

LUTHER.

The faith which brought us came from heaven ;
'Tis in us still, by mercy given.

Musicus.

Our notes are purer than of yore,
And rise and swell for evermore.

Epicus.

Our paradise through sin once lost
And once regained at boundless cost,
We trace our treasures to the cross,
For which we counted all things loss.
Now, as we walk this holy land,
(The harp of God held in the hand,)
We pour a rapturous minstrelsy;
Nor shall we to eternity
Cessation know of this our praise.
Our anthems are for endless days.

Choir of the Redeemed.

O Lord of all, whose mighty grace
Upheld us through our earthly race,
   And guided to this world above,
We bless Thy name.   Our constant lays
Can never utter all the praise
   We owe Thee for Thy boundless love.

We sought the grace for Thee to live,
And Thou to us didst freely give;
   We prayed in faith not once in vain;
The day of trial at an end,
No more could foes with us contend,
   No more our lot be grief or pain.

We live for Thee and do Thy will,
Receiving of Thy bounty still
   The strength that shall in us abide ;
This glorious life began below,
But more and more of Thee we know,
   And more as cycles onward glide.

Stupendous worlds that roll in space
Run in their paths a ceaseless race,
   To shew Thy power and work Thy will ;
And bird and fish and beast and tree
Their purpose serve and honour Thee ;
   And all things pure Thy aim fulfil.

In this fair land of love and peace
We dwell with Thee, and ne'er can cease
   To hymn the great Redeemer's praise.
Low at Thy throne, O Lord, we bow ;
Long hast Thou heard ; Thou hearest now ;
   And Thou shalt hear to endless days.

The wonders of Thy universe
We in our praises will rehearse,
   As worlds discover more of Thee ;
But that unutterable grace,
Whereby we stand before Thy face,
   Our endless joy-fraught theme shall be.

XVII.—HEAVEN.

— — —

Agnoscens dreams he hears in heaven the voice
Of God, the Father, Son, and Holy Ghost,
The acclaim of seraphim and the response
Of saints redeemed, of every nation, tongue,
And kindred of the earth, ten thousand times
Ten thousand.   Everywhere, below, above,
Around, are wonders.   " How," Agnoscens asks,
" Can I have found the way to this fair land,
The fairest in the universe of God ? "

——— ———

ANGELS.

God of all worlds that wheel in space,   .
    And run their never-ceasing race,
They move by Thee, and run Thy will to serve ;
    Author of life in man, in beast,
    In fish, in bird, all creatures feast
Upon Thy gifts, and Thou dost all preserve.

    God of all beauty, Thou dost see
    In tiny blade and stately tree,
In insect's wing, and light of central sun,
    Thy thought displayed in form complete ;
    And none can with Thy work compete
Or from Thy beauty-symbols ever run.

    God of all truth, Thy righteous will
    All creatures must for Thee fulfil

On earth below and in this heaven above ;
    But man, beloved and dowered by Thee,
    Hath plunged him in the stormy sea
Of sin, and may be lost in spite of love.

    God of all love, who giv'st him grace,
    He turns from Thee his guilty face,
And longs to live without Thy needful aid.
    Thou canst not let him pass away,
    Unwarned, unwooed, from light of day
To realms unblessed, for Satan's prison made.

    God of all good, thou canst restore
    Thy creature, that he sin no more,
But keep his feet in paths of truth and grace :
    Thou hast redeemed his soul from death ;
    'Tis by Thy gift he draws his breath ;
Canst Thou not turn the sad averted face ?

    Father of all, Thou touchest each ;
    Who wanders farthest Thou canst reach ;
Thou claimest all the race redeemed with blood.
    O'er earth's deep sin Thy servants weep ;
    They pray, and fast, and vigils keep,
In hope to stem the angry billowy flood.

    Who talk of truth but live in lies
    Must grope as those that have not eyes,
While round them streams the light Thy gospel pours.
    We wonder such a sight to see,
    And make complaint, O Lord, to Thee,
Whom evermore our being here adores.

GOD THE FATHER.

I speak in tempests through the trembling air
Of worlds, and in the wonders of the day,
The night, the great, the small. My witnesses
Are everywhere ; and man, made and redeemed
For me, can find no rest while he his face
Of guilt turns from My throne of righteousness.
Love rests upon My offspring, and the wealth
Of My approval has been offered all.
Man's nature, given by me, is chosen, best.
Perverted, it dishonours but itself,
Not Me, who fixed the limits of its strength,
In wisdom which no creature comprehends.
Men come to Me at my command or go
To please themselves ; and I firm balance hold
To give at length to each his own award. ·
This law of right is My eternal law,
And knows no change for evermore ; and all,
Or saved or lost, will bow to Me at length,
And own My judgments righteous all and true.

GOD THE SON.

My foes are conquered, and My name resounds
Through earth and heaven. Men hear it in their own
When they have ears to hear. The solemn march
Of years speaks it to them, their chronopher
The song of Bethlehem. The sheet that tells
The world's great story day by day repeats
My name in every tongue through every land,
Associate though it be with things profane,

Which it condemns with each returning dawn
My name will yet be seen by every eye
On earth, heard by each ear, and felt in all
The hearts of men.   I wait that every foe,
O'ercome, subdued, may own Me Lord of heaven,
Of earth, of hell, with humbleness and shame.
I wept when I beheld a city doomed
Because of sin ; and now My heart invites
The wand'rers home, all barriers once removed
By My atoning death.   The work complete
Makes plain the way.   Some walk therein and live ;
Some wander far and die ; but all are dear
To Me.   Over the lost My nature yearns,
As once I wept to see that city lost,
The city of my sires.   I died for all,
And live ; and all shall live that die to sin
For me, and take and bear my cross.   The rest,
Cast out and driven away from love's own home,
Are cursed by their own sin, but not by me.
My light shines everywhere, but some are blind
Because they will not see.   They close their eyes
And grope, boasting they know the way of life
And are the guides of youth ; they guide to death,
While such as follow Me walk home and live.
Speed ye, my messengers, on wings of love,
To warn and aid the race redeemed with blood,
Your joy to do My will and man to bless.

GOD THE HOLY GHOST.

The aims of thought divine are fathomless

To each created mind. I know them all,
And make them known as souls can bear to see.
Eternal love is guardian of man's weal,
And draws his heart to fellowship with truth.
Prayer is the fruit of My unceasing grace ;
The sense of sin were not without my touch ;
Nor penitence, should I withdraw My aid.
But all My work hath been denied by men
Whom vain deceits and proud philosophy
Led far astray.   In pain their victims writhe
And groan, pierced with the woes of pleasing sin
Which promised good but gave perpetual ill.
Delusions pass, and shadows flee away ;
The truth is substance, and shall ever stand,
To govern mind throughout the universe.
'Tis slowly seen by intellects obscured
With fogs and vapours of futility,
Which hide the facts of man's own consciousness.
It will be seen at length by every soul,
And, welcomed or repelled, bring joy or grief.
Ah, truth is soothing balm to souls at peace
With God and with themselves ; the heart at war
It bitterly afflicts ; but all will know
Its heavenly face before the destinies
Of men redeemed be published to the worlds,
And peace prevail through all the realm divine.
The creature sees not as Jehovah sees.
Yet man, how vain ! presumed to scan the ways
Of wisdom infinite.   That wisdom waits,
But not delays.   Meanwhile the heart of man

Is My demain, that I may prompt and guide,
Rebuke and intercede.   The penitent shall know
Himself, shall find the way of truth, and teach
His fellow man no more to stray in sin ;
And all shall know as also they are known,
Approving Heaven's unfailing purposes.

CHORUS OF ANGELS.

On ready wing
   We fly to earth,
And service bring
   Of countless worth
To heirs of life,
   Our joy to aid,
In pain or strife,
   Whom love hath made
God's servants true.
   O Master, we
Thy bidding do ;
   Our joyance see.
Deep in their sins
   The people sink ;
But Jesus wins
   Even from the brink
Of death.   (Pure love,
   Divine, immense !)
Below, above,
   A deeper sense
We gain of Thee,
   As through the land

Thy signs we see,
  And feel Thy hand.
What hast Thou done
  To save the race
By Satan won
  His lies to embrace ?
In love for man,
  (The rebel child,)
Messiah ran,
  Touched the defiled,
Nor could desist
  From His emprise
Even when death's mist
  Darkened His eyes.
For, lo, He bled
  On Calvary,
And bowed His head
  In agony,
To meet the case
  Of deep despair.
His work we trace,
  Known everywhere.
The grave was sealed,
  But Jesus rose,
And life revealed,
  In spite of foes.
The ransom paid
  For all the race
Shewed paths new-made
  For lives of grace.

To spirits poor
   The grace is given,
An open door
   Leading to heaven.
We know His will
   And love the way
That must fulfil,
   From day to day,
His kind behest.
   'Tis joy to us
When saints are blessed,
   And we haste thus
To help the best
   That dwell on earth.
O Lord of all,
   Who gav'st them birth,
On Thee they call
   For daily grace,
And long to see
   Thy smiling face.
May all agree
Thy perfect will
Quite to fulfil.

XVIII.—ETERNITY.

Agnoscens dreams he, wondering, stands
To look from heaven, and lifts his hands
At sight of earth, (that ancient home
Or prison, from which men could not roam,)
Enwrapped in flames ! Gazing, he waits
  While changes crowd.
  Uttered aloud,
This wondrous word his soul elates :
" The earth, the dwelling-place of men,
Destroyed, dissolved, is formed again,
The temple of all-holy souls."
While thus he lists, an anthem rolls
Through heaven, wherein are notes of praise
Such as men sang in distant days,
Such as the morning stars gave forth
When welcoming the new-born earth,
Such as become whom purest grace
Hath fitted for the heavenly place.

CHORUS OF THE REDEEMED.

We saw the saints all gathered home in peace,
The glorious harvest reaped of man's great race,
All foes subdued, all perils left behind,
All worthlessness cast out for evermore.

We saw Messiah's earth, dissolved, destroyed,
Rebuilt by hands divine, and decked in robes
Of everlasting youth ; nor heat nor cold,
Nor night nor sea, nor storm nor pestilence
Afflicting her free sons ; the curse of sin,
That all-corroding curse, by fire removed.
We saw the key of doom, (the Saviour's own !)
Its work done once for ever, thrown away,
To sink eternally in the abyss.
We saw, we felt, nor can forget, that day
Of days when doom was everywhere proclaimed,
And God's great purpose by all minds approved ;
Some souls, constrained, approved their own despair.
We have not seen them since, nor hope to see ;
But they are now where such are fit to dwell ;
Nor can we think one thought that gives us pain,
For ever perfect in this holy state.

    Our nature wonders more as more we know
Of God, revealed in worlds, but most in Christ,
Whose blood hath ransomed us, whose grace hath saved
Whose smile of love shall make our perfect heaven.
His call to worship we with joy obey,
Knowing His thought as it is meet to know,
Since not by tongues such as we heard in time,
Uncertain, slow, and tedious, and obscure,
Which sense concealed in deeps of changeful sound,
But by electric touch of speech divine,
Which works with thought and not with vocal breath
He calls us to adore.   Sweet pure delight
Is duty while our being, consecrate

To Him, thus homage pays, and He attends,
And of His grace our reverent service owns.
  O holy, holy, holy God, our Lord,
Thine are the treasures of the universe,
And we are Thine to serve Thy perfect will.
Servant to Thee is every world that moves
In the unfathomable realms of space,
And all that is pays homage to Thy throne.
In glowing suns Thy name is written large,
Since Thou in each dost utter Thy desire.
Thou art made known, in every part the same, ·
While systems speak Thy wonders infinite,
To fill the universe of mind with awe.
  Nor in minutest things art Thou unknown ;
For in the various leaf, the tiny grass,
The tinier flower that decked the waving field,
The insect which the eye could scarce discern,
And in the tiniest form invisible
Of life organic, could Thy name be read
By those who sought Thy grace that they might see.
But many looking saw not, being blind
To all that could be seen through grace alone,
Which they nor sought nor ever wished to see.
They proudly deemed They held the truth entire,
Forgetting that in facts the mind divine
Lay hid, to be sought out by humble souls.
  Long sat our race bound fast in error's chain,
Nor knew that liberty was love of truth,
Which freed the mind, defying prison walls.
The chain was forged by man's seducing foe,

And by a vain philosophy imposed.
How many saw, admired, and closer drew
That chain, and gave the name of liberty,
A sacred name, to licence foul. Even fiends
That shift deplore, its curse upon their heads.
Nations, deceived, long wallowed in the mire
Of vanity, whose stains were strangely prized,
Nor e'er removed by ministry of priests,
Who deemed themselves incarnate to absolve,
Though men absolved still lived the slaves of sin.
Rebelling evermore against Thy will,
Mankind, corrupted utterly, Thee, Lord,
Defied, and filled the earth with want and tears.
Thy enemies, O Lord, were everywhere,
Profane in boasting, vengeful in design,
Not seeing the futility of sin,
Nor hearing though Thou spak'st in thunder-tones,
Nor drawn by tokens of Thy boundless love,
Nor warned when Thou didst threaten direst war.
But Thou hast met them in Thy ways divine.
When love had waited long and could no more,
Vengeance, Thy liege, Thy last, came forth to fight
Against the foes of peace, of truth, of man,
To cast them down, for evermore destroyed.
    The call to arms, the din of strife, the groan
Of dire defeat, the shout of victory,
Then heard throughout the universe, are yet
Remembered well by all in heaven, in hell,
In realms of space. O'ercome, rebellion died,
With execrations loud, prolonged, and vain,

The universe left then in perfect peace ;
And never child of that fell sire shall wield
The sword again, since all confess Thee Lord,
The saved with joy, the lost with bitterness.
That conflict stands the last. No need for more,
Since it for ever teaches all that saw,
And all that hear the story told the worlds.

    Thy servants, Lord, from every age brought home,
Forgiven, renewed, and led, and glorified,
Will Thee obey, for ever in this realm,
In all that willing hands can find to do.
'Tis joy most pure to yield ourselves to Thee,
To bring in full the homage of the mind,
The burning love of consecrated hearts,
The glad submission of our steadfast will,
With all that makes our nature what it is.
Conquered by Thee and so true victors made,
We share Thy glorious conquest as our own.
With overflowing bounty satisfied,
In Thy full revelation we rejoice,
In Thy approval find our blissful heaven,
And in Thy grace go on to perfectness.
While cycles more than we conceive revolve,
Our joyful souls will turn, O Lord, to Thee,
In deepest rev'rence prostrate evermore.
Amidst the light that streams from Thy pure mind
We shall survey the wonders of Thy power,
And contemplate the grace which man redeemed
From lusts of vanity and ways profane,
To know Thyself, eternally approach

Perfection infinite, and grow in bliss
To endless days. That love which made us meet
In this pure world to dwell shall fill our souls
With songs of praise, and through our truth-tuned harps
Pour harmonies sublime, which Thou wilt hear
Approving, while with angel-minds shall be
Our fellowship. We give Thee praise, O Lord,
Because Thy word hath once for all made sure
Our perfect bliss, in perpetuity
Of converse pure. Thy word is ever true.
Thou speak'st, and we discern Thy perfect will,
Gladly, responsive, give Thee what is Thine,
And Father, Son, and Holy Ghost adore.

PAUL.

The strife hath ceased, but, Oh, it lasted long,
Hearts growing faint, waiting the glorious end.
I watched the conflict, taking my own part,
Nor could desist, constrained by love divine.
Now our Great Conqueror sits with glory crowned,
For ever Head of man's vast race of souls,
Prostrate before Him all created mind.
Wondrous that grace whose fruit I now behold,
And wonderful the story of our earth.
Yea, she hath seen her sorrows and hath groaned
With man and died, but with him risen again,
That she, remade, may live and testify
To all the worlds wherein are searching minds.
Let them learn wisdom from the tiny sphere
Whereon once walked the Truth, the Son of Man,

Words speaking which, we know, have been fulfilled.
Let all attend, and know His great design,
For He Revealer is in all the worlds,
The creature's Way to God, the Life of all
That live in these pure realms of spotless grace,
Of bliss which none in time could e'er conceive,
Of strength which is angelical, divine,
Since saints are one with Christ for evermore.
But envy is not in one holy mind.
All are content, and shall content remain, .
To see the favoured race teach all the worlds,
The new-made earth decked in her robes of grace
Peerless, supreme, that in her rays all minds
May read the perfect wisdom of their God,
Since o'er her fields the great Redeemer passed,
And she now shines the temple of His saints,
Witness of truth to all the circling spheres.

THE DREAM.

Agnoscens dreamed.   What is the dream ?
Solemn is life, whate'er things seem.
The dreamer dies ; his dreaming lives,
And counsel to survivors gives.
May they that ponder what he saw
In visions strange, survey with awe
The myst'ry of this passing life,
Wherein how many join in strife
With reason, conscience, law divine !
Be no such hapless conduct mine.
I would attain the wisdom sought
In prayer.   In love, 'tis sweetly brought
    To faithful souls,
      Whom truth controls.
'Tis shewn in all the paths of peace
Till death accords the sweet release.
O may I, like the dreamer, rise
To sing of grace beyond the skies,
To glorify in endless day
Jesus, the Life, the Truth, the Way.

ADIEU.

A stony road hath worn my weary feet;
 My hands at times have trembled at my side ;
 And some that started with me strong have died ;
But now, O Reader, we each other greet.
Oh, wherefore on this pathway should we meet
 Who never met before, and now must part ?
 If we have joined each other, mind and heart,
Can we, this journey ended, find it sweet
All to survey that we have said or seen ?
 No ; with the sweetness mingle bitter things
Which we deplore and wish we had not found.
Why through such mixture hath our journey been ?
 It is because, for thinkers as for kings,
Peace is not firm where truth is not its ground.

THE END.

EASTBOURNE:

WILLIAM GIVEN, PRINTER,

JUNCTION ROAD.